Thread on Arrival

"This is a great series with enough suspense and smart sleuthing to hook readers every time." —*Romantic Times*

"A fun, fast-paced mystery that will be hard to put down." —The Mystery Reader

The Long Stitch Good Night

"Lee's fourth Embroidery Mystery is well planned and executed. . . . Marcy's keen sleuthing and tenacious personality allow her to solve this solid mystery with smart thinking and style." —*Romantic Times*

"This series is smart and interesting, well patterned and deftly sewn together." —Once Upon a Romance

Thread Reckoning

"Lee's latest Embroidery Mystery will hook readers with its charming setting and appealing characters. Plenty of spunk and attitude follow Marcy as she solves this well-crafted mystery in a close-knit town full of colorful characters." —*Romantic Times*

Stitch Me Deadly

"The writing is lively, and the pop culture references abundant. . . . This book should appeal not only to embroidery enthusiasts, antique hunters, and dog lovers, but to anyone who likes a smartly written cozy that neatly ties up all the loose ends surrounding the murder but leaves the reader wanting to know more about the amateur detective, her friends, her life, and her future." —Fresh Fiction

continued . . .

"A well thought-out, free-flowing story that captures your attention and keeps you interested from beginning to end. The comfort of being in a craft store seeps through the pages as Marcy shows her sleuthing side to figure out the town's newest murders."

—The Romance Readers Connection

"There are plenty of threads for readers to pick up, and those who pick up the right thread will have the mystery sewn up in short order." —The Mystery Reader

The Quick and the Thread

"Lee kicks off a cozy, promising mystery series . . . a fast, pleasant read with prose full of pop culture references and, of course, sharp needlework puns."

—*Publishers Weekly*

"In her debut novel, *The Quick and the Thread*, author Amanda Lee gives her Embroidery Mystery series a rousing start with a fast-paced, intriguing who-done-it that will delight fans of the cozy mystery genre."

—Fresh Fiction

"Stands out with its likable characters and polished plot." —The Mystery Reader

"If her debut here is any indication, Lee's new series is going to be fun, spunky, and educational. She smoothly interweaves plot with her [main] character's personality and charm, while dropping tantalizing hints of stitching projects and their history. Marcy Singer is young, fun, sharp, and likable. Readers will be looking forward to her future adventures." —*Romantic Times*

Also by Amanda Lee

CROSS-STITCH BEFORE DYING

AN EMBROIDERY MYSTERY

AMANDA LEE

AN OBSIDIAN MYSTERY

OBSIDIAN
Published by the Penguin Group
Penguin Group (USA) Inc., 375 Hudson Street,
New York, New York 10014, USA

USA | Canada | UK | Ireland | Australia | New Zealand | India | South Africa | China

Penguin Books Ltd., Registered Offices: 80 Strand, London WC2R 0RL, England
For more information about the Penguin Group visit penguin.com.

First published by Obsidian, an imprint of New American Library,
a division of Penguin Group (USA) Inc.

First Printing, August 2013

ISBN 978-0-451-24007-1

Printed in the United States of America
10 9 8 7 6 5 4 3 2 1

PUBLISHER'S NOTE
This is a work of fiction. Names, characters, places, and incidents either are the
product of the author's imagination or are used fictitiously, and any resem-
blance to actual persons, living or dead, business establishments, events, or
locales is entirely coincidental.

The publisher does not have any control over and does not assume any re-
sponsibility for author or third-party Web sites or their content.

If you purchased this book without a cover you should be aware that this book
is stolen property. It was reported as "unsold and destroyed" to the publisher
and neither the author nor the publisher has received any payment for this
"stripped book."

To Tim, Lianna, and Nicholas

Chapter One

I was maneuvering my red Jeep down Main Street when I saw some sort of commotion up ahead. Angus, my Irish wolfhound, was in the backseat. We were on our way to the Seven-Year Stitch, my embroidery specialty shop, located in the Tallulah Falls town square.

I braked, squinted, and craned my neck; but all I could really see were the cars in front of me and the flashing lights of two police cars and an ambulance.

"Must be a car accident," I murmured to Angus.

As I debated trying to get out of the traffic so I could turn around and go another route to my shop, a woman on the street to my left screamed. I looked in the screamer's direction just in time to see a man dressed all in black shove past her. He was brandishing a handgun. The gunman hesitated, looked behind him, and then sprinted off again.

I, too, was anxious to see who was chasing him so I trained my gaze at the sidewalk and didn't watch to see where the man with the gun went. My heart dropped when I saw that the criminal was being pursued by Detective Ted Nash . . . *my* Ted. I closed my eyes briefly and said a silent prayer.

What could I do? How could I help? I couldn't just sit there.

I whipped my head around in time to see the gunman and Ted disappear around the corner. I desperately wanted to do something . . . anything. But if I distracted Ted and he was harmed because of my actions, I'd never forgive myself. As hard as it was, it was better for me to wait. Wait and pray. . . .

Suddenly, I heard the shots. They sounded no louder than firecrackers being discharged. *Bam! Bam! Bam!* Then silence.

Angus whimpered, aware that I was falling to pieces. He leaned over and licked tears from my right cheek.

I needed to get out of this traffic. . . . I had to park somewhere and see about Ted. The crowd had grown on the street, and, in addition to a couple of uniformed police officers, I thought I caught a glimpse of Manu Singh, chief of police. I knew he'd help Ted, but that reassurance did nothing to dispel my need to get to Ted and make sure he was all right.

I ignored the blaring of the car horns behind me as I edged out of the traffic and pulled onto a side street. There I parked, cracked the windows for Angus, promised him I'd be right back, locked the Jeep, and ran across the street.

"Let me through!" I shouted as I fought my way through the crowd. "Let me through!"

Someone had the audacity to stop me in my tracks. He was tall and strong, and I glared up at him. When I saw that it was Ted, I melted into his arms and sobbed.

"It's all right, babe." He ran his hands over my back tenderly. "It's all right."

I'd assured Ted I was fine once I'd seen that he was okay, and I came on to work. He'd wanted to drive me, but he had more pressing matters to attend to. He needed to go back to the station with Manu and question their robbery suspect. Fortunately, no one had been hurt when the man had fired off his weapon when leaving the bank with his bag of jewelry and cash—he was, thankfully, a lousy shot.

Now I tossed the bright yellow tennis ball from my spot on the sofa in the sit-and-stitch square into the merchandise area of the shop. It was a chilly, windy, cloudy day on the Oregon coast, and I hoped our morning of playing fetch would calm my jagged nerves and sufficiently tire Angus out. I wanted him to nap for a while so I could get some work done. I'd received a delivery late yesterday afternoon, and I hadn't even had time to open the box yet.

At a little over a year old, Angus was still a puppy. He loved to romp and play. He returned and dropped the soggy ball at my feet, and I tossed it again. This time it landed near Jill, and Angus nearly knocked her down as he retrieved it.

"Look out, Jill!" I called. Of course, she couldn't have moved out of his way anyhow. Jill was a mannequin.

The name of my embroidery shop was the Seven-Year Stitch, and the mannequin resembled Marilyn Monroe, who had starred in the movie *The Seven Year Itch*. So all day, day in and day out, Jill stood near the cash register silently greeting patrons to the store. She sometimes modeled some of my embroidery projects. For instance, today she wore a white, button-down oxford shirt with a cluster of crewel embroidery flowers on the left shoulder. Combining the shirt with her jean shorts, she looked fetching as she embraced springtime.

Many of my other embroidery projects adorned the walls—either framed or in embroidery hoops—

and I had candlewick-embroidered pillows on the sofa. Dolls dressed in clothing I'd embroidered stood on shelves throughout the store. I was not above putting embroidered bandannas around Angus's neck, but I didn't do it often since he didn't particularly go in for fancy accessories.

My cell phone rang. It was Mom. Mom, by the way, was the acclaimed Hollywood costume designer Beverly Singer. She lived in San Francisco . . . which was also where I'd lived until about nine months ago when I gave up a career in accounting to come to Tallulah Falls and open an embroidery shop. Mom probably thought I'd lost my mind at the time. But if she did, she never said so. She was awfully supportive.

"Hi, Mom," I said. "What's up?"

"I just got exciting news," she said. "Henry Beaumont has asked me to design and oversee costuming for a huge, lavish production about the life of early Bollywood star Sonam Zakaria."

"Congratulations! That's terrific. Tell me all about this guy Sonam and why Mr. Beaumont is making a movie about his life."

"Sonam was a *she*, darling, and she was larger than life. The only American star I can think of to even remotely compare her to off the top of my head would be Elizabeth Taylor," Mom said. "Anyway, this job is going to be quite an undertaking. And since the studio has given me an extremely generous budget, I'd like to hire you and a few of your most trusted stitchers to help me out."

"Are you serious?" I asked.

"Absolutely. I'm afraid I won't be able to do it without you." She paused. "Wait. That's not fair. I'm sorry. I'd *love* for you to help with the costumes, but I understand if you're too busy. I can—"

"Mom, I want to help," I interrupted. "And I'm sure Vera will." Vera Langhorne was a widow in her late fifties to early sixties who was always game for a little adventure.

"What about Reggie?" Mom asked. "She's so skilled in chikankari that she'd be ideal for this project. Do you think she'd be willing to pitch in? If nothing else, maybe she could give the rest of us a crash course in Indian embroidery."

"I'll call her and ask," I said. "I'll let you know as soon as I talk with her."

"Thank you, dear. Give my love to Angus and Ted."

"About Ted. . . . He had quite the adventure this morning." I told her about our earlier excitement.

"Oh, darling, I'm so glad he's okay! What a terrible ordeal. Are you all right?"

"I'm still a little shaky, but I'm getting over it," I said.

"With all this going on, are you sure you want

to take on a stitching project of this magnitude?" she asked.

"Of course. They caught the guy. Everything is fine now."

"If you're sure. . . ."

"I'm sure. I'll talk with you later. Love you, Mom."

"Love you more than chocolate," she said.

We ended the call, and I smiled at Angus. "That was Grandma," I told him. "She loves us more than chocolate. Yes, she does!"

He woofed, scooped up the tennis ball, and took a run around the shop with it.

Before I could call Rajani Singh, better known as Reggie, my friend Sadie MacKenzie came in and was nearly bowled over by Angus. Sadie had been my best friend since our college days. She and her husband Blake owned MacKenzies' Mochas, a hip little coffeehouse down the street from the Seven-Year Stitch. In fact, it was Sadie who'd convinced me to move here and open my shop.

"What's got him so excited?" Sadie asked, as she walked over to join me on the sofa facing away from the window in the sit-and-stitch square.

The square was so named because two navy sofas faced each other with an oval maple coffee table between them. On either end of the coffee table were two red club chairs with matching ottomans. A red-and-blue braided rug beneath the coffee table pulled everything together and created a cozy square where customers could come sit and stitch.

"We've had an exciting morning," I answered Sadie. "First we saw Ted chasing an armed man on the street, shots were fired, and I nearly had a breakdown. Then Mom called."

"I heard about the robbery and the chase afterward. Was anyone hurt?"

"No."

"That's a relief. So what's your mom up to?"

"She's signed on for a *huge, lavish production*— her words, not mine—about some Bollywood starlet. Mom has asked me and some of Tallulah Falls' finest needle crafters to help with embroidering the costumes."

"Have fun with that." Sadie was so not a stitcher.

"I should take you to San Fran to the movie set one day to be an extra," I said. "Mom could get you in."

"I don't think I could be an extra on a Bollywood movie."

"With a scarf and veil, you could."

"With a scarf and veil, *you* could," she said.

"Not me. I'm way too pale. I read something cute the other day on some blog forum." I grinned as I quoted, "We Oregonians don't tan; we rust."

She smiled. "That is cute. Oh, hey, Todd took

Audrey Dayton out to dinner last night." She carefully watched to gauge my reaction. "I haven't heard from him this morning—he didn't even come in for his usual espresso—so I don't know how it went."

"I'm sure it went great," I said. "I'm the one who suggested they'd make a good couple in the first place, remember?"

"I remember. I only wanted to make sure you hadn't had a change of heart now that . . . you know. . . ." She shrugged. "He seems to be getting over you and moving on."

"Sadie, nothing could make me happier. Ted and I are so right for each other. I see it more and more every day, and I believe he does too. I wish you could see it."

Since I'd first arrived in Tallulah Falls, Sadie had been trying to fix me up with Todd Calloway. Todd owned the Brew Crew, a pub and craft brewery directly across the street from the Seven-Year Stitch. Todd and I went on a few dates, but it never amounted to more than friendship. Sure, Todd was sweet and good-looking, but I never felt the spark of excitement with him that I felt with Ted Nash, head detective for the Tallulah Falls Sheriff's Department.

I felt Todd had been hurt when I chose Ted over him, but it was probably more from pride than anything else. Like me, Todd realized that though we cared about each other, it was as friends. And while the idea of Todd getting seriously involved with MacKenzies' Mochas' mean-spirited waitress Keira made my stomach churn, I was delighted that he and the kind, auburn-haired deputy Audrey Dayton might be compatible.

"You know, I suspect Todd didn't come by for his usual espresso this morning because he was avoiding Keira," I said.

"That's a pretty safe bet. She was livid when she found out he and Audrey had a date. She thought that with you out of the picture, she was all set." Sadie smiled. "Maybe Blake and I can have you and Ted over for dinner sometime soon."

"That would mean a lot to both of us," I said. *Especially since you've made it apparent that you thought our relationship was a mistake.* I didn't say that last part out loud, of course . . . only in my head.

As soon as Sadie left, I called Reggie. Reggie was the librarian for Tallulah Falls' only public library. I could tell by the clipped efficiency of her voice when she answered the phone that I'd called her at a busy time.

"Hi, it's Marcy," I said. "I won't keep you, but I'm calling to ask if you'd be willing to help out my mom with some Bollywood costumes."

I didn't need to explain anything further. Reggie knew my mom from the times Mom had visited Tallulah Falls, and all my friends had enjoyed listening to her "war stories."

"That sounds fantastic," Reggie said. "I'll be over to the shop on my lunch break to get all the details."

As I'd hoped, Angus spent most of the late morning napping by the window while I attended to customers, opened the box that had been delivered yesterday afternoon, and restocked the pegboards with embroidery hoops and frames. The merchandise area of the shop was separated from the sit-and-stitch square by a black-and-white checkerboard tile floor. I'd worn heels today, and they clicked on the tile as I placed the canvas and monk's cloth on the maple shelves, refilled the bins with yarn and embroidery floss, and put the overflow in the storeroom. Normally, that clicking sound combined with our being alone in the store would've made Angus come bounding over to jump and nip at me. Today he was too worn out from the earlier game of fetch.

Once my work was caught up—for the moment—I returned to the sit-and-stitch square and felt pleased with myself for a job well done. I glanced up at the clock and saw that it was a quarter until twelve.

I went into my office and made sure there were

sodas in my mini-fridge. After Reggie had told me she'd be by around noon, I'd called and asked Ted to bring us a pizza for lunch.

I heard the bells over the shop door jingle, and I hurried out of the office. I was glad to see that Ted had not only brought the cheese pizza I'd asked for, but that he'd also brought Reggie's husband, Manu.

They were quite a contrast standing there side by side. Ted was six feet, three inches tall, dwarfing Manu, who stood a mere five feet, seven inches. Not that I was one to talk about height. At five feet nothing, Manu dwarfed *me*.

Ted was muscular and athletic. Manu was muscular, too, but he had a stockier build. And while Manu had deep-set dark brown eyes, Ted's eyes were as blue as the ocean on a clear summer's day.

I greeted Ted with a quick kiss. "This is a nice surprise," I told Manu.

"When you said Reggie was coming over, I thought we should make it a foursome," Ted said.

"I'm glad you did," I said.

Angus, who'd loped over when the men first walked in, was busying himself trying to sniff at the pizza box that Ted was holding up out of the dog's reach.

"You'll get your share, buddy," Ted said.

"Especially after Reggie gets here," Manu added.

"I'll grab us some paper plates, napkins, and sodas," I said.

Ted and I usually ate in my office; but since Manu and Reggie were joining us, we'd need to dine in the sit-and-stitch square.

When Reggie arrived, I put the cardboard clock with the plastic hands on the door indicating I'd "be back" in half an hour. I didn't lock the door, but I hoped any customer who might come by during that time would respect our desire to eat lunch uninterrupted.

As we ate, I explained about Mom's new project and advised Reggie that Mom had requested her specifically because she did such gorgeous chikankari work. Reggie was sporting some of that white-on-white embroidery today on the fitted cuffs of her cream-colored tunic. Unlike her husband, who favored Western dress such as jeans and plaid shirts, Reggie preferred her traditional Indian attire of flowing tunics with matching pants or saris.

"I'm flattered that your mother thinks I'm good enough to be of help," Reggie said, lowering her head in modesty and pushing her silver wire-framed glasses up on her nose.

"Good enough?" I scoffed. "She wants you to give the rest of us—including her crew in San Francisco—a crash course!"

"I'm looking forward to seeing this movie,"

Manu said. "Sonam Zakaria was an incredible talent."

"Yes, she was," Reggie said. "But she had such extreme highs and lows in both her career and her personal life. Who will be playing her in the movie?"

"I don't know," I said. "I didn't think to ask Mom when I was talking with her."

"Will you have to go to San Francisco?" Ted asked, tossing a piece of pizza crust to Angus.

"I should go at least overnight to get a feel for the designs and what Mom will need," I said. "But most of our actual work will be done here. Reggie, I'd love for you to go with me to San Fran. How about this coming weekend? Maybe we could all go."

"I'd like that," Reggie said.

"Great. I'll check to see if Mom thinks it's a good idea. If she does, I'm sure the studio will pay for our flight, and we can stay with her. We could try to get a flight out right after work tomorrow evening and. . . ." I noticed the guys were looking at each other. And although I couldn't read their expressions, I knew Ted well enough to realize that one or both of them would not be going to California. "What?"

"Ted and I can't go," Manu said. "Our robbery suspect escaped this morning."

"Escaped? How?"

"He punched the deputy who was cuffing him,

and then he got away," Ted said. "He apparently ran through one of the shops and out the back where we think there was a car waiting."

"You believe he had an accomplice?" I asked.

"He would have had to have," Manu said. "He got away too easily."

"We're thinking he must've hidden in the trunk or the back floor and that his driver simply merged into the traffic and fled the scene while we were still combing the shops for our suspect," Ted said.

"Oh, my goodness. That's terrible." I placed my hand over Ted's. "I'll call Mom back and ask her to get someone else."

They all spoke at once.

"No, you won't," said Ted.

"Over my dead body," Reggie chimed in.

"That's not necessary," Manu said. "We'll catch this guy . . . hopefully before the sun sets today."

"Still, I don't think it's appropriate to leave and go to San Francisco," I said.

"It's a perfect time to go," Ted said. "If we don't catch this guy, Manu and I will be working around the clock to find him. You and Reggie might as well enjoy yourselves."

I turned to Reggie.

She shrugged. "He's right. Let's go. We won't do them any good by pacing the floors and wringing our hands at home. Trust me—I've been there and done that."

"Besides, somebody has to babysit." Ted inclined his head toward Angus.

"Our men are too busy for us this weekend, Marcy," Reggie said with a wink. "We might as well skip town."

I smiled uncertainly. "I'll make the arrangements."

Chapter Two

After lunch, I called Mom. "Reggie is on board," I said. "In fact, she and I want to visit you this weekend so we can get a better feel for the project." I had no intention of worrying Mom with the fact that the gunman Ted had pursued this morning had escaped. I might tell her over the weekend during our visit if he hadn't been recaptured by then, but not now.

"That's wonderful. I was thinking of coming to you, but your coming here will be much better. You and Reggie can visit the set, meet with Henry and some of the other cast and crew members, and Reggie can show my in-house embroiderers some of her chikankari work," she said. "When will you be here?"

"I haven't made the travel arrangements yet—I'll do that as soon as we're finished talking—but we hope to leave right after work tomorrow."

"Great. Of course, the studio will reimburse your travel expenses. You'll be staying here with me, won't you?" she asked.

"As if I'd stay anywhere else," I said.

"I knew *you'd* be staying with me, but I wasn't sure about Reggie. Do you think she'll be comfortable here?"

"I didn't ask her, but I believe she'll be perfectly comfy in the guest room. By the way, Ted and I had lunch with Reggie and Manu today. The two of them knew all about Sonam Zakaria and are looking forward to seeing the finished movie."

"That will certainly please Henry," said Mom. "He's been worried that a movie set in India might not play well in the United States. Naturally, I reminded him of the successful reception of *Slumdog Millionaire*."

"Naturally," I agreed. "Reggie and Manu wanted to know who Henry cast in the starring role, and I had to admit I have no idea."

"Remember Babushka Tru from the sitcom *Surf Dad*? She was the youngest daughter."

"I remember that show," I said. "She was so cute! Didn't she go on to play in a couple of family films?"

"She did. And then she got involved in drugs and made a mess of her life. She's hoping this movie will be the blockbuster she needs to get back on Hollywood's radar."

"Is she nice?" I asked.

"I haven't met her yet. I'm supposed to meet with Henry and the cast in the morning to discuss wardrobe."

"Well, good luck."

She huffed. "I might actually need it with this crew."

As soon as I'd finished talking with Mom, I made travel arrangements for Reggie and me. We were going to fly out of Eugene. It would have been a little cheaper to fly out of Portland, but Eugene was closer. Besides, the studio could afford the extra couple hundred dollars we were spending on the flights, especially since we were flying in business class and saving them a bundle over what they were used to paying for first class. After making the arrangements, I sent a text to Reggie giving her the details.

A customer came in and bought several skeins each of pale pink and white yarn. Her daughter was expecting twin girls, and she was knitting blankets for them. I congratulated her and gave her fifteen percent off.

"It'll be my gift to the babies," I said.

"Thank you," the woman said. "I'm sure I'll be back in to see you soon."

As she waved good-bye and left the store, I

thought that if her daughter was anything like my friend Riley Kendall, the woman would be back in often over the next few months. I remembered how many things I'd made for Riley while she was pregnant with her daughter Laura. She'd commissioned me to embroider bibs, blankets, and even burp cloths. And I believe Riley enlisted every knitter in Tallulah Falls to knit white blankets for the child.

Riley was one of the busiest attorneys in town. When she'd gone back to work after Laura's birth, she had simply taken the baby with her. Since Riley's administrative assistant was her mother, the situation worked out especially well.

I was planning on calling Vera as soon as I got time, but then I looked up and saw her strolling through the door.

"You must have ESP," I told her, as she bent down to hug Angus.

"Not ESP, dear. If anything, I have OLD. I can't for the life of me remember how to make a Colonial knot."

When I first met Vera, she was a rather matronly, mousy-looking woman with a husband who'd never fully appreciated her. Since his death, she'd blossomed into a confident, self-assured woman. She dressed more fashionably, had added blond highlights to her brown hair, and had become a pro at makeup application. She was in her late fifties to early sixties, but her transformation had taken at least ten years off her appearance. She'd recently begun dating Paul Samms, a reporter for the *Tallulah Falls Examiner*.

"Well, come and sit down with me, and I'll remind you about Colonial knots . . . after I tell you my news—actually, it's *your* news too, if you want it to be." I took her by the arm and ushered her over to the sofa facing away from the window.

"You'd better spill before I burst," she said, taking her seat. "At first, I thought you were going to tell me that Ted had proposed. But I don't know what that would have to do with me."

"It's a little early in our relationship for that, don't you think?"

She shrugged. "You never can tell. So what *is* your news?"

"Mom has taken a job where she's going to need lots of embroidery help," I said. "She's asked me to enlist the aid of Tallulah Falls' finest stitchers, and you're one of the first people I thought of."

Vera's eyes widened. "Seriously? You're asking *me*? I just told you I can't even remember how to make a Colonial knot."

"One, I'm going to refresh your memory on those Colonial knots, and you'll be doing them like you've been making them all your life. Two, I doubt we'll even have to make Colonial knots for this project. And three, you'll get paid and might even get to visit the movie set."

Although I knew she didn't need the money—her parents had left her a small fortune—Vera loved prestige.

"Will we get to attend the premiere?" she asked. "With all those stars? And the paparazzi?"

"It could happen," I said. I didn't really have a clue. Nor did I have a desire to attend the premiere. But if Vera did, I was pretty sure Mom could pull some strings and make it happen.

Vera clasped her hands together and gazed up at the ceiling. "Paul will definitely want to do a piece on us for the paper."

"That would be great." I bit my lower lip. "Before we get to that Colonial knot, do you know anyone off the top of your head who could watch the shop for just a little while on Saturday? I'm going to San Francisco."

"You're going to San Francisco?" she asked, lowering her eyes to meet mine. "Is it about the film?"

I nodded. "The film is about a Bollywood star named Sonam Zakaria, so Reggie and I are going to visit Mom to learn what we'll be doing. We'll probably bring some things back with us, so we can go ahead and get started on the embroidery."

"This is so exciting," she said. "Will we be learning that Indian embroidery Reggie does?"

"More than likely. I'm hoping it's similar to either candlewick embroidery or crewel . . . something everyone is already fairly familiar with."

"So tell me more about the movie," Vera said. "Who will we be costuming?"

"Mom said the film's star is Babushka Tru. She was a child star and is hoping to make a comeback with this movie."

"I remember Babs. She was that adorable pre-schooler from *Surf Dad*."

"That's her." I tried to gently prod Vera back to answering my question. "About Saturday. . . ."

She flicked her wrist dismissively. "I can handle the shop. Don't worry about it."

"I can't impose on you that way, Vera. I thought maybe you knew of some college kid or someone who could use a few extra bucks and wouldn't mind being here for the day."

"It's no imposition. Thanks to you, I'm going to take part in making a movie." She smiled. "You never know, they might even let me be an extra or something. This is so fun and exciting. I'll be glad to watch the shop. Just show me how to work the register, and Angus and I will take it from there."

"Well, you don't have to stay all day. And I'll pay you—"

"You will not," she interrupted. "And of course, I'll stay all day. The more people who come in, the more people I can tell I'm getting ready to work on a movie." She grinned. "You can bring me a loaf of sourdough bread, though. There's nothing like sourdough from San Francisco."

"Consider it done. Thank you so much."

"Thank you for letting me be a part of costuming stars," she said. "By the way, does Angus need a sitter while you're gone?"

"Nope. Ted has to work this weekend, so he's taking care of him."

"Have Ted bring him by the shop on Saturday morning. The pup can hang out with me while Ted is busy. Besides, the regulars would be disappointed if he wasn't here."

I gave Vera a quick hug. "You're the best."

"I know. Now hurry up and show me how to make a Colonial knot so I can go tell Paul that I'm—I mean, *we*—are in the movie business."

Though I typically taught embroidery classes on Tuesday, Wednesday, and Thursday evenings, I'd given the spring session's Thursday slot to help a domestic abuse victims' group learn to do cross-stitch and needlepoint. The members of that class had recently completed their projects and had moved on to beading, so my Thursdays were now free until summer. I was glad about that . . . this evening, in particular. I needed to pack, plus I wanted to enjoy some time with Ted before I left.

This would be the first weekend since we began dating that we'd be apart. Sure, we'd only been together for six weeks, but still. . . .

I decided to make him a nice meal. On one of our first dates, he'd made chicken piccata for me so I thought this time I'd make him something Italian. I mentally scanned the contents of my pantry and fridge. I had all the ingredients for lasagna. Plus, I could run out to the grocery store after dropping Angus off at home and get a loaf of garlic bread and the ingredients for a tossed salad. And I knew just what to make for dessert.

What had started out as a boring, overcast Thursday had quickly become an exciting day.

Angus and I arrived home at around five fifteen. I let him romp in the fenced backyard while I ran back out to the grocery store. Afterward, I hurried upstairs to shower and change. Once I was dressed and had finished fussing with my hair and makeup, I went back downstairs, set the oven to preheat, and got out my favorite peanut butter cookie recipe. I hadn't made the cookies in years, so I hoped they'd be as tasty as I remembered.

I quickly mixed the flour, brown sugar, butter, vanilla, egg, and crunchy peanut butter together and then formed the cookies on the cookie sheet. Like any experienced peanut butter cookie maker,

I flattened them slightly with a confectioners' sugar-dipped fork. Still waiting for the oven's preheating indicator light to go off, I placed the cookie sheet on the counter and began preparing the lasagna. I was browning the ground beef and waiting for the water for the pasta to come to a boil when I heard a click telling me the oven was ready. I placed the cookie sheet into the oven and continued my lasagna preparations.

By the time the cookies were done, I was ready to layer the lasagna. I placed the cookie sheet on a wire rack and layered the lasagna ingredients into the long, rectangular pan. I placed the pan into the hot oven and set the timer.

The cookies weren't really cool enough to eat yet, but I had to try one to make sure it would be good enough to serve to Ted. If they weren't good, I'd planned to serve ice cream and not mention the cookies. I tried one. Oh. My. Goodness. They were so good. Warm . . . gooey . . . yummy. . . .

I opened the back door. "Angus, come here! You have *got* to try these cookies!" Sometimes it's so great to have a best buddy on hand to share things with.

He came galloping in to oblige me. I put a cookie into his bowl and he virtually inhaled it.

I didn't have a formal dining room, but my kitchen was huge. The cabinets were pine, and I'd found an ash square table and four chairs that matched them perfectly. My dishwasher, refrigerator, and microwave were white. And I had blue granite countertops.

For this evening's dinner, I'd placed a light blue linen tablecloth and napkins on the table. In the center were two single silver candlesticks with white taper candles—lit, of course, after I'd let Angus go back outside. I'd sliced the bread and had it in a bread basket with a warming trivet in the bottom. A bottle of Sangiovese was chilling in an ice bucket near Ted's place setting.

When Ted arrived at around seven, I met him at the door. I was wearing a lacy black top and white slacks.

"Wow," he said. "Something smells wonderful."

I playfully punched him in the arm. "You were supposed to say, 'Wow. You look great.'"

"You *do* look great." He smiled. "And you smell wonderful . . . and whatever you're cooking smells terrific, and. . . ."

"Okay, that'll do." I stood on my tiptoes and pulled his head down to mine for a kiss. "I made lasagna and peanut butter cookies."

"Where's Angus?" Ted asked.

"He's in the backyard. He's already given his seal of approval to the cookies. I'll save him some lasagna, and we'll let him in after we eat," I said. "I wanted our meal to be uninterrupted."

He kissed me again. "I like uninterrupted."

"I know you do." I took his hand and led him to the kitchen.

"Any luck finding the gunman?" I asked.

He sighed and shook his head. "The night shift is following up leads. I'll stop by there on my way home and see if they've dug up anything new."

I hugged him. "I think that was the scariest thing I'd ever experienced this morning—you disappearing around the corner with that guy . . . hearing the gunshots. . . ." I shuddered.

"Let's not think about it. I don't want it to spoil our evening. Plus, I'm starving."

Chapter Three

Before I went to work the next morning, I packed for the trip to Mom's house. The first thing I put into my suitcase was a pair of my coziest cotton pajamas. Staying with Mom always meant a night of vegging out to old movies, hot cocoa, and fun conversation.

Next went the jeans, T-shirts, cardigans, and scarves. The mantra for packing for a trip to San Francisco was *layers, layers, layers*. I also packed a skirt, a pair of dress pants, and a pair of nude heels to wear for meetings with Henry Beaumont and other cast and crew members.

I was filling my toiletry bag when Mom called.

"Hi," I said. "I was just—"

"Wait until you meet that nasty little piece of work," Mom interrupted.

"Who?" I asked.

"Babushka Tru—or Babs, as she's more com-

monly known . . . or even BTru in the tabloids."
She emitted a growl of frustration. "I just came
from my initial meeting with her and some of the
other actors. I was afraid a couple of the cast might
be a bit full of themselves, but not her. I expected
her to either be kind of like she was as Sylvie in
Surf Dad or at least a bit more respectful."

"Mom," I said gently, "you know that actors are
rarely—if ever—anything like the characters they
portray."

"Of course, I do. But I also know that with her
history of drug and alcohol abuse, petty theft,
showing up late or not at all when scheduled to be
on the set in more recent films. . . ." She huffed. "I
simply thought that if she truly wanted to show
Hollywood that she'd finally grown up and was
ready to become a respected young actress that
she'd at least be polite."

"So she didn't treat you with any respect whatsoever?" I asked.

"Not me, not the hairstylist, not the makeup
specialists, not the production manager, not the
key grip . . . not anybody! She was even short with
Henry."

"How did he react to that?"

"Nauseatingly," she said. "The way he sweet-
talked and pussyfooted around her behavior,
you'd have thought she was the hottest A-list star
in Hollywood rather than some little has-been!"

"I've not heard you this upset over a project in a long time. Are you still doing it?"

"Yes." She huffed. "Henry and I go back a long way. Plus, the rest of the cast and crew is fantastic. And—it's all merely rumor and speculation at this point—but there are people in the know who are whispering about a little golden statue."

I wasn't quite sure what to say about that. Mom worked hard, and I'd love for her to win a major award like that, but I didn't want to get her hopes up . . . especially if she found that she and Babushka Tru couldn't work together after all. So I said, "Mom, if anyone deserves that award, you do. But I really have to get to the shop. We'll talk more when Reggie and I get to San Fran this evening."

"Hopefully, I'll be over all this frustration by then. Thanks for letting me vent, darling. I'll be at the airport to pick you up."

Angus and I made it to the shop at just before ten a.m. I hated cutting the store opening that close. I liked to be there fifteen to thirty minutes before the shop was scheduled to open so I could double-check all the supplies were adequately stocked, that everything was neat and tidy, and that Jill looked presentable. After all, she had been nearly knocked down by Angus yesterday. Something like that could even shake up a mannequin. I also liked to have the coffee brewing so its warm, inviting aroma would welcome customers as they stepped into the Seven-Year Stitch. This morning, I had to go through my routine *after* opening up the shop. I just hoped my patrons wouldn't be early birds today.

Wouldn't you know it? As soon as I had that thought, the bells over the door jingled to let me know someone had arrived. I was in my office readying the coffeemaker, so I called out, "Good morning! I'll be right with you!"

"How about I come to you instead?" My visitor spoke from the office doorframe where he leaned casually with his hands in the front pockets of his pants.

"That suits me." I finished emptying the container of water into the coffeemaker and then went to wrap my arms around Ted's neck.

He pulled his hands from his pockets and drew me to him for a deep kiss. The kiss was, of course, interrupted by a scruffy gray face wedging its way between us.

"Watch it, mister," Ted told Angus. "I'm going to be your caretaker for the next two days. You don't want to get on my bad side."

Angus looked up at Ted, giving him a dopey doggy smile.

Ted scratched Angus's head. "I know, buddy. You're gonna miss her too."

"What brings you by so early?" I asked. "Not that I'm complaining in the least. . . ."

"I won't be able to have lunch with you today," he said. "Manu and I are driving to Lincoln City to talk with the sheriff there about robberies similar to the ones we're investigating here. We're hoping his staff might have some leads on our gunman and his partner."

"Good luck."

"Thanks. We'll need it."

I frowned. "Please be careful."

"Always, sweetheart." He blew out a breath. "This is frustrating. But we'll get this guy . . . and his accomplice . . . eventually."

"I know you will." I kissed him softly.

"Manu and I will be back this afternoon to take you and Reggie to the airport."

"Great. I'll look forward to seeing you then."

As he left to go get Manu, I wondered about the robber that had befuddled the two brightest law enforcement minds in Tallulah Falls. Ted hadn't talked much about the case to me prior to the encounter I'd witnessed yesterday. He'd only told me the thief was very clever and was using technology skills to hack into people's smartphones and laptops to steal their identities. He was also targeting victims and copying their safe-deposit box keys in order to get into their boxes. The people were carefully handpicked, since the thief knew exactly what he'd be getting.

The Tallulah Falls branch of the Metropolitan Bank Group had notified police when they suspected something wasn't right yesterday morning. Although the thief had disguised himself to look like the person whose box he was opening, the bank manager was a personal friend of the victim and had known this wasn't him. He slipped away and called the police. By then, the robber had fled with several pieces of heirloom jewelry and over a hundred thousand dollars in cash.

I poured myself a cup of coffee and took my laptop into the sit-and-stitch square. I brought up my favorite search engine and looked up *chikankari*.

I learned from one Web link that references to the Indian embroidery technique dated back as early as the third century BC and was also known as *chikan*. Stitches included in chikankari work were flat stitches, which remained close to the fabric; embossed stitches, which presented a grainy appearance; and jail work—seriously, *jail* work—which provided a delicate netting.

Another Web site debunked my belief that chikankari was solely white-on-white embroidery. Instead, it appeared to be white-on-any-color embroidery. Blues, yellows, and pinks were particularly lovely. The site also informed me that there were six basic stitches used in chikankari and that all but one were used in other types of embroidery. There were eyelet stitches, chain stitches, darning stitches, and stem stitches.

Yet another site advised that chikankari was very delicate and time-consuming. This site advised that it typically took ten to fifteen days to embroider a single outfit.

One thing was for sure—chikankari was absolutely nothing like candlewick embroidery. I desperately hoped Reggie would be able to teach the technique to me and to the other Tallulah Falls stitchers so we'd be able to adequately help Mom. Maybe . . . hopefully . . . it wouldn't be as complicated as it appeared to be. Sure. . . . That's why one Web site stated that the stitches involved in chikankari were so elaborate that there were specialists for the various groups of stitches. What had I gotten myself into?

In a panic, I called Reggie. She assured me everything would be fine. But suddenly, I had a terrible feeling about this entire project.

After MacKenzies' Mochas' lunch rush, I called Sadie and asked her to come over and watch Angus and the shop for a few minutes while I took care of a couple last-minute errands.

"Getting a little present for your mom?" she asked.

"No, but that's an excellent idea," I said. "She was stressed out when I spoke with her this morning. Maybe I can find her something cute. By the way, could you bring me half a dozen of those blondie brownies Ted likes so much? I'll pay you for them when you get here."

When Sadie arrived, I paid her for the brownies and put them in my office. Angus seldom wandered into my office when I was in another part of the shop, but I put the treats out of his reach in case their aroma proved to be too enticing for him to resist.

"Need anything while I'm out?" I asked Sadie.

"Not that I can think of."

I told her to call me if she thought of anything and that I'd be back as soon as possible. I didn't think my errands should take more than thirty minutes, but I didn't supply Sadie with a specific return time other than to tell her I'd hurry. "If something comes up and you need to leave, just lock the door and put that little clock thingy on it saying I'll be back in half an hour, okay?"

"Okay." Sadie stepped behind me and began propelling me toward the door. "If you don't go on, we'll be having this discussion at closing time."

I realized she was right, promised again to make it a speedy trip, and then I left. My first stop was the pet store where I got Angus the peanut butter dog biscuits he enjoyed so much. Then I went to the market and got Ted his favorite trail mix and gourmet coffee blend. He and Manu would likely be working all hours, and I wanted them to have some tasty goodies on hand to make it seem less tiresome.

I stopped by the local florist's shop and ordered a rainbow bouquet of roses to be sent to Vera to thank her for working at the shop and looking after Angus tomorrow. When I saw how beautiful the bouquet was, I decided to call a florist in San Fran and order the same bouquet for Mom. I hoped it would cheer her up even before Reggie and I arrived.

When I returned to the Seven-Year Stitch, Sadie was eager to see what I'd been so anxious to buy. She peeped into the pet store bag. "Peanut butter biscuits?"

"He loves them." I took the bag from Sadie, reached in, and pulled out the box. They were the doggie equivalent of the cookies I'd made Ted.

Angus immediately started hopping about expectantly.

"See?" I opened the box and gave him one of the treats. "Just one, young man. You and Ted shouldn't eat all your goodies at once and gorge yourselves simply because you're living the bachelor life this weekend."

"You're really crazy about him, aren't you?" Sadie asked.

"Of course, I am! He's my fuzzy bear! Aren't you?"

Angus merely chewed and wagged his tail. Notice how he didn't speak with his mouth full? Good manners.

"Not him," Sadie said. "Ted."

I smiled. "Yeah . . . I guess I am."

Todd Calloway, the Brew Crew owner that Sadie had once hoped I'd fall madly in love with and vice versa, dropped in later that afternoon while I was poring over some articles on chikankari I'd printed out. He started a game of fetch with Angus and then sat beside me on the navy sofa facing the window.

"What're you doing?" he asked, furrowing his brow as he looked down at the intricate embroidery on the page I was holding.

"Frankly, I'm beginning to think I've bitten off more than I can chew and am wondering if I can discreetly spit it out." I explained about Mom, the movie, and the crash course in Indian embroidery.

"You'll be fine," he said. "I have confidence in you. Besides, anything they need to show up close, they'll have Reggie do. Right?"

"I'm so glad you have such confidence in me."

He laughed. "I do. It just has its limits."

Angus returned with his tennis ball, and Todd gave it another toss.

He was cute—Todd, I mean. He was no Ted Nash, mind you, but he wasn't without his charms. He had chocolate brown eyes, wavy brown hair, and one of the warmest smiles you could imagine.

"What brings you by?" I asked.

"Sadie told me you were going away for the weekend, and I wanted you to let Ted know that I'm willing to help look after Angus while Ted's at the station."

"That's really thoughtful. Thanks." Everybody loved Angus. "But Vera is going to mind the shop tomorrow, and she insisted on having Ted bring him by to stay with her."

"You're leaving Vera in charge of the Seven-Year Stitch?" he asked with a grin. "Are you sure that's such a good idea?"

I shrugged. "She volunteered and seemed happy to do it. She'll be fine. I hope she gets a lot of traffic. She's looking forward to telling people she has a role in costume creation for an upcoming movie."

"By the time you get back to Tallulah Falls, the story will have grown from her having a small role in costuming to having the starring role in the film." Todd laughed. "Good thing you're not taking her to San Francisco, or she'd be begging Ricky to put her in the show."

"She's not Lucy," I said, giving him a wry smile.

"What's got you in such a punchy mood today? Is it some other redhead you have on your mind other than Lucille Ball?"

He looked around. "Where'd Angus go? We were right in the middle of a game of fetch."

"He went to lie in the sun," I answered. "Now . . . 'fess up. How are things going with Audrey?"

"We went out to dinner the other night, and it wasn't a disaster."

"It wasn't a disaster? Is that the best you can do?"

"For now," he said. "I'm taking things slow."

"Taking things slowly is good," I said. "Just don't move too slowly."

He tilted his head. "Good point. I'd hate to fool around and let some other guy beat me to the punch . . . again."

Awkward. "Audrey seems sweet," I said.

He nodded as he stood. "I'd better get back to the Brew Crew. Have fun in the big city."

I smiled. "There's never a dull moment with Mom around—that's for sure."

Chapter Four

It was wonderful to see Mom waiting for Reggie and me at the gate. I'd barely had time to put my carryall on the floor before she'd gathered me into a bear hug. It was incredible that a woman who looked as sophisticated and refined as Mom could squeeze a person that hard.

I laughed. "You look terrific." She'd had summery highlights added to her medium blond hair and had it cut to delicately frame her face. Other than that, she looked as she had when Ted and I had visited a few weeks ago. "I love your hair."

"Thanks." She brushed a strand of it off her shoulder. "This was Stefan's idea. He's the head hairstylist on set. This is my first time working with him, but I adore him. He's a genius." Mom turned to Reggie and gave her a more conservative hug. "How are you, dear?"

"I'm great," Reggie said. "Thank you for having

me as a guest in your home and for including me in this cool project."

"You're welcome at my house anytime," Mom said. "As for the project, don't thank me until you've met Ms. Shrew . . . I mean, *Tru*." She glanced at her watch. "Come on. We have to get your luggage and get to the restaurant. We're meeting Henry at Le P'tit Laurent."

I hated that we didn't have time to run by Mom's house and freshen up before going to dinner. I supposed retouching my makeup in the car would have to do.

As we drove to the restaurant, I reiterated to Mom how scared I'd been yesterday morning. "You can't imagine the panic I felt when Ted chased that guy around the corner, and then I heard gunshots."

Mom took one hand off the steering wheel to pat my arm. "I'm so sorry, darling. I'm surprised you even came to San Fran after that. But it's all right now, isn't it? They caught the man."

I flipped down the visor and lifted the cover of the vanity mirror so I could apply my lipstick. Reggie was sitting in the backseat directly behind me, and I noticed her eyes dart from left to right. "Actually, the man escaped."

"Escaped? How?" Mom asked.

"The deputy was handcuffing the suspect," Reggie said. "He'd clasped on one of the cuffs, but the suspect elbowed him in the stomach and then whirled around to head butt him before he could get the other one fastened. Officer Childress was knocked unconscious. By the time his partner and Manu reached him, the suspect was gone."

"So this crazy person is on the loose, and he knows Ted can identify him," Mom said.

I hadn't thought about that.

"I don't think he'll hang around Tallulah Falls," Reggie said. "He's facing multiple felony charges. He wants to be as far away from Ted as he can get."

"But what if Mom is right?" I asked. "What if he stays and tries to hurt Ted because Ted can identify him?"

"He won't," Reggie said firmly.

"It was my fault that the man escaped, wasn't it?" I sighed. "If I hadn't gone running over to make sure Ted was all right, the suspect would still be in custody."

"You don't know that," Reggie said.

"Yeah . . . I think I *do* know that."

Le P'tit Laurent was located in Glen Park. Glen Park was close enough to Miraloma Park, where Mom lived, that I was still a little put out that we couldn't swing by the house to freshen up before meeting Henry at the restaurant. Of course, Le P'tit Laurent was extremely popular and required advance reservations, and Mom knew me well enough to realize that my "freshening up" would turn into an hour of changing clothes, washing my face and redoing my makeup, and fussing with my hair. So she was smart to drive us straight to the restaurant where Henry was already waiting at an intimate corner table.

I'd dined at Le P'tit Laurent before, but I was struck anew at the elegance of the French eatery. The gleaming dark hardwood floors provided a stark contrast to the pristine white tablecloths, napkins, and dinnerware bearing the restaurant's name in red. The table was set with crystal stemware, and Henry looked as if he was more than ready to use his wineglass.

He was as distinguished looking as you might imagine a Hollywood producer-director to be. His dark hair had grayed at the temples, and he had clear blue eyes . . . tonight. Sometimes his eyes were brown, sometimes green, sometimes violet. . . . He was a big fan of colored contact lenses.

He rose from his cane-backed chair when we approached the table. "Bev, you look lovely," he said, as he pulled out her chair. "You too, Marcy."

"Good to see you again, Mr. Beaumont," I said. "This is Reggie Singh. She's an expert at Indian embroidery."

Reggie and Henry exchanged pleasantries as we sat down.

"Have you seen Laurent this evening?" Mom asked Henry.

Laurent Legendre was the owner of the restaurant, and he took a very hands-on approach to running the place. He often greeted and conversed with diners.

"He came by about ten minutes ago—just after I got here," Henry said.

"I'm sorry I missed him," Mom said. "But if I know Laurent, he'll be back."

I grinned. "If he realizes you're here, he will be. If nothing else, he'll come over so you can tell him for the umpteenth time that he looks like that French football player. . . . What's his name?"

"Didier Deschamps," Mom answered. "And Laurent *does* resemble the man." She chuckled. "But let's get down to business. I've already told Henry that you, Reggie, and a few of your friends will be helping the costuming department out with the extensive embroidery that needs to be done."

"Yes, and I'm especially glad to have you on board, Reggie," Henry said. "Not only will you be able to contribute your own embroidery skills, you can serve as a quality adviser on the rest of the work—making sure it looks authentic and up to par."

"Oh, I don't know about that," Reggie said. "I'm not here to critique anyone."

"But if not you, then who?" asked Henry. "You're an expert on the craft, and you can ensure the veracity of the workmanship. You've seen it all your life, correct?"

"Well, yes," she said.

"All right then." Henry gave a nod of satisfaction and dismissal.

Reggie was saved from further commenting when the waiter arrived to take our order. I could tell by the way she was fidgeting that she felt nervous and out of her element, but I also knew she'd be fine when she got used to the movie people. There was no way she'd let any shoddy work go out on her watch.

We each ordered our food, and Henry asked for a bottle of Château de Seguin to be served while we were waiting on our food. I felt tired from working all day and then traveling, and I certainly didn't need a glass of wine to exacerbate that feeling. But I didn't want to appear rude, so when the waiter returned, I accepted a glass, sipped it, and commented on its robust flavor.

"So how is everything coming along with the film?" I asked.

"Almost everything is going swimmingly." He took a deep drink of his wine.

"Is there a problem with the cast?" I could hear

the hopeful note in Mom's voice as she posed the question. I knew she'd love for Henry to say that Babushka Tru wasn't working out.

"No. The cast is fabulous," Henry said. "I'm just not a hundred percent satisfied with the set for Somwarpet. That's the town where Sonam Zakaria was from."

"I'm familiar with Somwarpet," Reggie said. "It's a quaint little town."

"So you've actually been there?" Henry asked.

Reggie nodded. "Often. In fact, there's a heavily wooded area on the outskirts of Tallulah Falls that reminds me of Somwarpet."

"Really?" A slow smile spread across Henry's face, and he took his cell phone from his jacket pocket. "Excuse me, ladies."

I had a feeling Reggie and I would have some company on the flight home.

After dinner, Reggie, Mom, and I went to Mom's house. Too tired to unpack, I simply washed my face, put on my pjs and slippers, and went in search of Mom.

The house I grew up in was gorgeous. Other than furniture (rarely) and accents (often), Mom didn't change much about the home. She never felt the need to redo the color scheme or tear out the kitchen for a full remodel. That's why, no matter how long I was away for at a stretch, the house was constant, familiar, and comforting. The house was a Victorian, built in 1920 and completely upgraded before Mom and Dad bought it in 1975.

I found Mom in her office. The room was the perfect blend of sophistication and glamour that Mom had not only infused into our home but into her personal style as well. The heavy burgundy velvet drapes framing the window behind her glass-topped desk were pulled back and held with a tasseled gold cord. Ebony cabinets and shelves lined the wall to the right of the desk and gleamed in the light emanating from the crystal chandelier hanging in the middle of the room.

I sank onto the wine-colored sofa with the gold fleurs-de-lis, and I sighed.

Mom looked up from the notebook in which she'd been writing. "In order to be more dramatic, dear, you should throw your wrist across your forehead when you sigh like that. What's up?"

"I'm just tired."

She scoffed. "I know there's more to it than that."

"I'm concerned about this project," I said. "On the one hand, I'm thrilled with the prospect of being able to help you out. On the other hand, I'm afraid my work won't meet the demanding expectations of Babushka Tru . . . or the awards committee, for that matter."

"Oh, I don't give a fig about the diva *or* the awards committee." She angled her head slightly. "I care less about Babs than I do the committee, but I have no doubt you'll do a fantastic job. So you have nothing to worry about." She frowned. "It's not like you to get so nervous over a new adventure. After all, you left everything you'd been familiar with here and moved to Oregon without any qualms whatsoever. What's got you so worked up about helping with costumes on this movie?"

"I'm really not sure." I shrugged. "I just have this feeling of foreboding."

She scooted back her chair and came to give me a hug. Sitting beside me with one arm still around my shoulders, she said, "I think what you're really worried about is Ted . . . because that gunman escaped."

"That could be part of it. I'll call him in a few minutes and make sure he and Angus are doing all right. Still, there's something about this movie—something about Babs—that concerns me. I'm afraid this project won't end well."

Mom gave me a one-armed squeeze. "You let me worry about Babs. I can handle whatever she throws at me."

I hoped that was true. But my sense of unease didn't go away.

*   *   *

By the time Reggie and I had awakened and got ready to go on Saturday morning, Mom had already been down to Creighton's and bought us some delicious ham and cheese croissants for breakfast. We didn't have time to linger over them, though. The studio beckoned.

When we pulled up to the guard shack, Mom passed along an extra croissant to Bertram, a stocky, older gentleman who'd been the gatekeeper there for the past twenty-five years. He gratefully accepted the treat and, with a wink, pushed the button that raised the white metal bar and allowed us into the studio.

"Henry is working at soundstage two today," Mom said. "It's where most of the indoor shots for the movie are being filmed."

She parked the car, and we strode to the cavernous building that housed the interior sets for the movie, currently titled *Sonam Zakaria: A Glamorous Life*.

The red light indicating filming was taking place inside was off when we arrived, and Mom took Reggie and me onto the set. We picked our way over cables, around cameras, and through scurrying groups of people to stand quietly and watch the cast going through their lines.

Although this was merely a rehearsal and the actors weren't in costume, it didn't appear to me that Sonam Zakaria's life had been all that glamorous. Since Babushka Tru wasn't in her movie makeup, I couldn't tell if the scene being rehearsed had taken place at the beginning or the end of her career. The set was a seedy-looking hotel room. The furniture was cheap and unattractive, and the wallpaper was peeling. Had this been the actual room rather than a re-creation, I'd have expected it to smell musty and stale . . . maybe smoky too.

Before we could observe very much of the scene, Henry called for the cast and crew to take a thirty-minute break. He turned with an exasperated sigh, but smiled when he saw us.

"Beverly, Marcy, Reggie!" His voice boomed across the room, and I was embarrassed when just about everybody turned to look at us. "Come over and meet Babs!"

Babs, who'd been stalking away, turned only when Henry caught her by the arm. She rolled her large dark eyes and flipped her long black hair over her shoulder. "I met the seamstress yesterday, Henry. Remember?"

"She's the costume designer, darling, and I want you to meet a couple of the women who'll be embroidering your fabulous saris and tunics," he said.

"Why?" she asked, her voice flat and bored.

"Because it would be a nice thing for you to do." Henry spoke softly, but the acoustics were terrific, and we heard him as if he'd been standing directly in front of us rather than halfway across the room.

"I don't feel like being nice right now," Babs hissed. "Tell the sewing machines I'll catch up with them later."

Mom said nothing, but I could tell she was seething when she gave me a pointed look that clearly said, *See what I mean?*

Swishing her hair over her shoulder again, Babs left Henry standing alone. He looked embarrassed when he came to join us.

"Babs isn't feeling very well right now," he told us.

"No problem," I said. "Mainly we're just here to get Mom's sketches and some of the clothing we'll be working on for the shoot. We didn't mean to interrupt you."

Henry smiled at me warmly. "You're a welcome distraction."

"I imagine so," Mom said.

"What do you mean?" Henry asked, his smile fading.

"Only that the scene we were watching looked pretty intense," I said, meaning the one *after* the scene that was supposed to be in the movie.

"Exactly." Mom gave Henry a tight smile. "I get the feeling this is going to be a labor-intensive project for all of us."

"You *are* up to the task, aren't you, Bev?" he asked.

"Of course I am," Mom replied confidently.

"By the way, I'm going to send a couple land-scape and photography scouts with you and Reggie to Tallulah Falls tomorrow, Marcy," Henry said. "If they agree that the area will work for us, we'll begin filming there as soon as possible."

Reggie grinned at me.

I only wished I could share in her and Mom's excitement over this project.

Chapter Five

It was late Sunday afternoon when the small plane carrying Reggie, me, and Henry Beaumont's two handpicked experts touched down in Eugene, Oregon. I'd called Ted to alert him to the change in Reggie's and my travel arrangements. He and Manu would still be picking us up, of course, only they'd be doing so two hours earlier than they'd previously anticipated. The guys were thrilled about that; and, despite the fun we'd had over the weekend—for the most part—Reggie and I were thrilled to be getting home early too.

We hadn't had any more interaction with Babs, Henry, or anyone else connected to the movie after our visit to the studio Saturday morning. We'd merely picked up our materials and moved on. But, like Mom, I felt this was going to be a very labor-intensive—and for her, uncomfortable—project to be a part of. Mom was tough, and I knew she could outlast Babushka Tru if she put her mind to it. I just hoped Babs didn't give Mom too much trouble. After all, Mom was successful. She could gracefully bow out of this project and be working on another movie set the next day. I kind of wished she would.

After visiting the studio, we'd taken the clothing back to Mom's house and then went to Point Bonita Lighthouse. We'd hiked and picnicked, and Reggie had taken tons of pictures. Sunday morning, we'd just relaxed and chatted with Mom. Mom had invited some of her assistants over for lunch, and Reggie had given them a crash course on chikankari. They caught on very quickly— much quicker than I did!

Upon touching down in Eugene, Reggie and I got off the plane and hurried to the gate. Manu and Ted met us with flowers. Manu had brought Reggie's favorite stargazer lilies, and Ted had a dozen red roses for me. I barely avoided crushing them when I launched myself into his arms.

"I've missed you," I said. "How's Angus?"

"He's fine, but we've both missed you like crazy," Ted answered. "He's gonna be thrilled to see you."

I grinned. "I'll be happy to see him too. Did you catch your robbery suspect?"

"Excuse us for interrupting," said Sonny Carlisle, the burly, dark-haired movie locations manager. "Ron and I are going to go on over and pick up our rental car." Ron was tall, slender, and balding; but his open smile and mischievous green eyes gave him an air of attractiveness and approachability.

"Please forgive my rudeness," I said, horrified that I'd forgotten the two men in my excitement over being home. "Guys, this is Sonny Carlisle and Ron Fitzpatrick, locations manager and director of photography for Henry Beaumont's upcoming movie. Sonny and Ron, this is Ted Nash and Manu Singh."

The men shook hands and exchanged pleasantries.

"We'll wait for you to get your car, and then you can follow us to Tallulah Falls," I said to Sonny.

"That's not necessary," he said. "We've got our GPS, and we'll be fine. We'll meet you and Reggie in the hotel lobby in the morning at eight."

"All right." I smiled. "See you then."

I didn't revisit the subject of the robbery suspect until Ted and I were in the backseat of Manu's white Ford Bronco headed back to Tallulah Falls.

"You guys were getting ready to give Reggie and me an update on your gunman when Sonny and Ron interrupted," I said.

"Were we?" Ted met Manu's eyes in the rearview mirror.

"There isn't much to update," Manu said. "We've been following every lead, and police departments all across Oregon and our neighboring states have a description of our guy. But he seems to have gone underground. We'll simply have to wait him out."

"You don't think he'd try to find either one of you. . . . Do you?" I asked.

"No way," Ted said with a chuckle. "He's avoided capture for this long by being smart. It isn't likely he'll suddenly go stupid on us." He put his arm around me and drew me close. "So how's Bev?"

With a sigh, I rested my head against his chest. "I really wish she'd pull out of this project. I've got a terrible feeling about it."

I was having a major battle with my conscience over having to leave Angus while Reggie and I met with the locations experts and took them to the site the next morning. I cupped the dog's large head in my hands. "I shouldn't be more than an hour, and then I'll be right back to get you. I promise."

Angus whimpered as if he didn't believe me. I almost relented and took him along on the scouting expedition then; but I wasn't familiar with the area we were visiting, and I didn't know how

Sonny and Ron felt about dogs. So I reiterated my promise and tried to avoid his eyes as I slipped out the door.

Before I could back the Jeep out of the driveway, Angus pushed aside the curtain at one of the living room windows and pressed his nose against the glass. It was adorable. I caved.

I put the Jeep in park and rushed to unlock the front door. "Come on, Angus," I said.

He nearly ran over me getting to the car.

When I got to the Inn at Tallulah Falls, I cracked the windows and hurried inside. Reggie was already standing in the rustic, ski lodge–inspired lobby. I was surprised to see that she was wearing jeans, though her top was a traditional Indian tunic.

"Good morning," I said. "This is different. I've never seen you in jeans before."

She smiled. "This is the only pair I own. I wear them when Manu and I go hiking."

"So when you said this place was remote, you weren't kidding."

"Not by a long shot," she said. "It makes Point Bonita look tame. I hope our friends are up to the trek."

"I hope *I'm* up to it. By the way, I brought Angus along. Do you think they'll mind?"

She shook her head. "They're movie people. Surely they've worked with animals before."

"I could probably slip in a snarky jab at Babushka Tru here, but I'd better not," I said.

"Will your mom actually have to work all that closely with Babs?" Reggie asked.

"I'm afraid so. I just don't know how much of her abuse Mom will be able to take."

The elevator doors opened and Sonny and Ron stepped out.

"Hi, ladies." Sonny greeted us in his booming voice. Ron merely raised his hand in a cordial wave.

"I hope you don't care that I brought my Irish wolfhound along," I said. "I figured I'd just follow you guys in my Jeep since I don't know where we're going anyway. Plus, it might be good to have him along on a hike."

"Oh, I love dogs," Ron said. "Can I ride with you?"

"Of course," I said.

Sonny turned to Reggie. "Then, Mrs. Singh, please lead the way."

Reggie was driving Manu's Bronco; and as I followed it out of town, I chatted with Ron. I learned that he had two dogs—a beagle mix and a chocolate Labrador retriever. And he told me that he had an ex-wife and one child—a son—and that he'd worked with Henry Beaumont for the better part of fifteen years.

Of course, I really wanted to ask him about Babushka Tru, but I knew I'd have to broach that topic carefully.

"Has it ever been difficult for you to work with someone on a particular movie set?" I asked.

"I get along fine with most people," he said. "When I cross paths with someone whose personality doesn't gel with mine, I find it's best to simply avoid that person."

"But what if you can't? Then what do you do?"

Ron sighed and turned in his seat to pet Angus. "Look, Marcy, I know what you're getting at. Everyone on set is aware of how your mom feels about Babushka Tru. None of the guys seem to have a problem with Babs. And while the other women in the cast and crew don't particularly *like* the girl, they all know they'll have to work with her." He turned back to face the front. "Actresses have the reputation for being divas—for throwing tantrums, being disrespectful, showing up at their leisure, making constant and often ridiculous demands. . . . They're not all that way, of course, but the behavior of those who are is more widely tolerated because they fill cinema seats."

"Costume designers don't," I said, finishing the thought he'd left unsaid.

"Not so much, no. Don't get me wrong—your mother is an important cog in the machine."

"But she's not the star."

"She's not the star . . . and, as far as I know,

there aren't any rumors about your mom and Henry," he said.

I whipped my head around to look at him before turning my attention back to the road. He was looking down at his hands.

"Babushka and Henry?" I asked, my voice emerging as a screech. "But she's young enough to be his daughter, and he's *married*."

"It could just be unfounded gossip," Ron said. "You know how people like to talk . . . especially when they don't know anything. I'm only telling you because I'd hate to see your mom lose this job. If she can't work with the situation as it now stands, tell her to get out while the decision is hers to make."

I mumbled a *thank you* as I noticed that Reggie had pulled off the road. I followed and parked on the shoulder behind her.

She got out of the Bronco and came to my side of the Jeep. "We'll have to hike the rest of the way."

I grabbed Angus's leash, got out of the Jeep, and opened the back door. Angus shifted over to allow me to snap the leash onto his collar, and then he bounded out to greet Reggie.

"Hi, baby," she said. "Ready to go for a walk?"

Angus wagged his entire body.

Ron slung his camera bag over his shoulder. He wore one camera around his neck; and before we began our ascent, he took the lens cap off and started snapping photographs.

As we climbed the rocky path that led to Tallulah Falls' answer to Somwarpet, India, Reggie led the way, Sonny walked as closely to her as possible, Ron trailed behind them, snapping shots all the way, and Angus and I brought up the rear. We must've presented a strange parade to anyone watching.

Not that I'd have thought anyone *was* watching until someone whizzed past on a dirt bike. The bike came out from behind a thicket of brush and had to swerve to miss Reggie. She jumped out of the way and would have fallen had Sonny not been there to catch her.

I hurried forward. "Reggie, are you all right?"

"I'm fine." She pushed her hair out of her face and her glasses back up onto the bridge of her nose. "I was just startled." She pointed. "The area I was telling you about is right up ahead."

I could see that Reggie had been embarrassed by her reaction to the dirt biker, but that biker had come dangerously close to hitting her. The biker had been wearing heavy clothes and a dark, face-hiding helmet. And the biker had been alone. I didn't think it was a swell idea for anyone to be in such a remote area alone. I made a mental note to ask Ted if this was a popular dirt biking spot. If so, and if Sonny and Ron found this to be a good set location, they might need to hire extra security to keep the bikers from coming onto the set—accidentally or otherwise.

When we got to a clearing, Reggie explained that the wooded area surrounding it had always reminded her of Somwarpet. "The only thing missing is Abbimatta Falls."

"We can edit that in," said Sonny, surveying the area both critically and appreciatively. "This sure comes closer to the pictures we've seen than anything in California. Don't you think so, Ron?"

"Absolutely." Ron spoke from behind his camera and amid the whir of photos being captured. He eased the camera bag off his shoulder, opened it, and took out a tripod. "I think this is it. We need to get Henry out here so that if he agrees, we can move on it."

Sonny nodded. "In the meantime, we can go to the courthouse to see who owns the land and go through the proper channels for permission to film." He looked at Reggie. "Is this place in the town or the county?"

"Tallulah County," she answered and then went on to give him directions to the courthouse.

"When we get back to the hotel, I'll upload these pics and send them to Henry," Ron said. "Sonny, you can handle the legalities."

*   *   *

Ron rode with Reggie and Sonny back to the hotel, so Angus and I could go straight on to the Seven-Year Stitch. For some reason, the incident with the dirt biker was really nagging at me, so I called Ted and asked him if it was a popular hangout.

"I can see why kids might like the thrill of that rocky terrain, but no one should be out there alone," he said. "That's a dangerous area. I'll check with the county officers and see what they say about it."

"Okay," I said. "Thanks."

"Hopefully, I'll know something by lunch," he said. "What are you in the mood for?"

"I could really go for a chef's salad."

"I could go for a chef's salad between two slices of rye."

I laughed. "I think they call that a club sandwich, don't they?"

"Something like that," he said.

After talking with Ted, I called Mom and asked her how things were going. It was only midmorning. I hoped things couldn't have gotten too bad already. They had. Mom launched into a tirade about Babs and how spoiled she was and how she didn't have any decency in her whatsoever.

"Furthermore, she doesn't have an ounce of acting ability," Mom said. "I don't know how in the world she got this job."

"Have you heard any rumors . . . about Babs and Henry?" I asked.

Mom was uncharacteristically quiet.

"Are you there?" I asked, afraid the call might've been lost.

"Yes. I'm just processing your question. It isn't a random one, is it? Someone said something."

"One of the locations experts," I said. "He told me to tell you that if you can't work with Babs to leave now."

"Before they throw the old broad out and ruin her reputation?" Mom spat the question out of her mouth as if it were poison.

"He didn't say that in so many words. . . ."

"But that was the gist, yeah, I get it."

"Mom, I'm only telling you this for your own good. I have a bad feeling about this entire project."

"I appreciate your concern, Marcella, but I will be completing this project. I'm in for the long haul. I'll prove myself to that guttersnipe if it kills us both. I'll talk with you soon, darling. Good-bye."

With that, she was gone. But that wasn't the last I'd heard of killing that morning. About an hour after I'd first spoken with Ted about the dirt bike incident, he called to tell me that the Tallulah County Police Department had gone up to investigate whether or not there were dirt bikers trespassing along the trail. I hadn't considered that we were trespassing this morning, but there were more important issues to think about.

The officers hadn't found trespassers, but they had found the body of the gunman who'd shot at Ted. The biker who'd nearly hit Reggie was more than likely the person who'd killed him. Lunch was canceled. Ted and Manu were on their way to assist in an examination of the crime scene.

Chapter Six

Given the fact that Mom was determined to continue on with the movie, I began working on one of the costumes in between customers. I had been given a sky blue tunic which I was to embellish with chikankari around the neckline, hem, and cuffs. Thankfully, this particular tunic called for a simplistic design. It was for one of the low points in Sonam Zakaria's life—either during her late childhood or after her first divorce. I felt it was a good starter piece for me.

I used a washable fabric marker to freehand the design onto one of the cuffs. I decided I'd begin with the wrists. The fabric on the cuffs was a little heavier and would better tolerate my ripping out the stitching if I wasn't satisfied with the work and had to start over.

I was sitting in the sit-and-stitch square working on the cuff when Reggie came by the shop.

After kissing Angus on top of the head, she flopped onto the sofa across from me and sighed.

"Uh-oh. You look like you have bad news," I said.

"Not bad really . . . just not great. Ted told you the gunman they've been looking for was found dead near the location we visited this morning, didn't he?"

I acknowledged that he had. "He also said it's likely the biker we saw killed the gunman."

"Yeah, he and Manu think the two of them were partners and that they'd met there to work out a new plan or to divvy up their loot or something," she said. "What concerns me is that Sonny Carlisle stopped by the library earlier and told me that Henry loved the location and is eager to use it."

"Why is that bad?" I asked. "Did the owner of the property refuse them permission to film on the land?"

"No, but the land has been cordoned off with police tape. It's an active crime scene."

"So, now what? Is Sonny scrapping the location?"

Reggie shook her head. "Oh, no. Right now he's at the county sheriff's office trying to persuade them to let the film crew work around the crime scene."

"I don't really see that happening," I said. "Do you?"

"Manu certainly wouldn't let them, but I don't know what the Tallulah County Police Department will do."

We didn't have to wait long to find out. Reggie had gotten up to leave when my cell phone rang.

"Wait," I told her. "It's Mom."

Reggie sat back down as I answered the phone.

"Rally the troops," Mom said. "We're headed your way."

"What?" I asked.

"Henry just called and told me to be ready to fly to Tallulah Falls in an hour. I'm packing as we speak."

"Hold up. Has Henry spoken with Sonny? Does he know the area meant to become Somwarpet is now a crime scene?"

"Only part of it has been designated a crime scene," Mom said. "And the police department will have officers protecting that secure area around the clock. We have to get our Somwarpet scenes shot as soon as possible . . . which is why I need for you to get me and my assistants some stitching help."

"Of course. Reggie is here now, and I'll call Vera. I know she'll be excited about this turn of events." I paused. "Is Henry *sure* the police chief is okay with him filming there now? I mean, the investigation should be concluded within a few days, and—"

"Trust me," Mom interrupted. "The police chief is fine with the shoot. Henry has promised the department a new computer system and the chief's daughter a walk-on."

When I called Vera with the news that we were going to have to begin our work sooner than we'd originally expected, she was delighted.

"This is so exciting," she said. "Paul is having to write nearly nonstop to keep on top of it all. Did I tell you he came by the shop on Saturday and took a few photographs?"

"I believe you did," I said, remembering how she'd gushed about Paul's visit and the article he'd planned for a special Wednesday feature when I'd spoken with her last night. "I'm looking forward to seeing the piece in Wednesday's *Chronicle*."

"So am I. And I'm glad he'd already written it up because, of course, the big story today is that body the police found on the outskirts of town."

"Of course," I said. "Mom and the necessary cast and crew are on their way to Tallulah Falls now. Can you be here at ten thirty tomorrow morning to get started?"

"I'll be there with bells on," Vera said.

Knowing Vera, she might actually show up wearing bells.

Ted came by just as a group of bridesmaids were leaving the Seven-Year Stitch. The women were going to make a quilt for the bride as a wedding present. Each of the five women was making ten squares, so it would be quite a sizable quilt when they got it sewn together.

Ted held the door for the women as they departed, and I saw more than one throw an admiring glance his way. He either didn't notice or pretended not to as he walked on into the shop and dropped a light kiss on my lips.

"That must've been a sizable sale. I counted five customers, and they all had more than one bag." He grinned. "Does that mean you can knock off early today?"

"Actually, I am going to have to leave at about four thirty." I glanced at the clock—it was three forty-five. "I have to pick Mom up at the airport. Henry is flying her and some other members of the cast and crew here in his private jet."

Ted's smile faded. "Manu and I heard that Beaumont was going ahead with the filming."

"I can hardly believe that the Tallulah County Police Department is letting him do that," I said. "Surely Henry could wait until the crime scene was processed."

"You'd think so. But the county's crime scene techs are pulling an all-nighter trying to completely scour the area so Beaumont can begin setting up tomorrow."

"An all-nighter? Tired crime scene technicians are bound to miss something."

Ted flipped his palms in a gesture of helplessness and then moved over to the sofa facing the window. Angus came to sit on the floor beside him, and Ted absently scratched the dog's head as he spoke. "The county guys allowed Manu and me to do some investigating of our own. We weren't able to find much other than the same types of things recovered by their techs: smartphones, credit cards, and a few tablets and laptops hidden near some dilapidated buildings on the property." He blew out a breath. "Their guys are good, and their initial search was thorough and impeccable. But it's like you said, once they're twelve hours into their shift and they're exhausted, the investigation will suffer."

"I feel sorry for the crime scene people. It's unfair for the police chief to do them that way simply to accommodate Henry Beaumont's shooting schedule." I sat down beside Ted. "Until today, Henry didn't even have Tallulah County *on* his shooting schedule."

"Yeah, well, I guess that's how it goes when you have a fifteen-year-old daughter who dreams of being the next Babushka Tru," Ted said.

"You heard about that, huh?"

He nodded. "And the new computer system too."

"Well, at least, there will be officers on hand to

secure the crime scene and to provide another level of protection," I said.

"I wouldn't put too much faith in that extra security, Inch-High."

Despite staying up until after one a.m. talking with me, after Ted dropped us off following dinner the night before, Mom was wide awake and raring to go by eight o'clock Tuesday morning. She was in the kitchen making breakfast when I went downstairs.

I kissed her on the cheek before I sat down at the table. "You seem to be feeling happier than you were when we went to bed last night."

She put a cup of coffee in front of me. "I'm not sure *happier* is the word I'd use. It might be better to say that after sleeping on it, I'm more accepting of the situation." She shrugged. "I came to the conclusion that I need to either scrap the project or come to terms with Babs."

"And you're not about to let some no-talent diva knock you out of the running for an Oscar?" I asked.

She grinned. "You've got it." She hurried back to the stove to flip the pancakes she was making. "How many of these can you eat?"

"Two," I answered.

"That's what I was guessing. Angus has already had his and is outside running them off."

"Them? Mom, how many did you give him?"

"Only two," she said. "Although he *is* a growing boy."

We ate, and Mom insisted on cleaning the kitchen back up while I went up and got dressed. She was being very sunny and domestic, and I hoped she wouldn't have a run-in with Babs that would change her demeanor from June Cleaver to Meat Cleaver.

We got to the Seven-Year Stitch at about a quarter before ten. Mom fluffed the sofa cushions and neatened the yarn and floss bins as I readied the coffeepot and called Vera and Reggie. Vera informed me that she would "report for duty" within the hour. Reggie, however, would be unable to make an appearance until lunchtime.

"I never dreamed we'd be needed so quickly," Reggie said.

"Neither did I," I said. "Mom just arrived last night."

"I can try to take tomorrow off, but I can't promise anything. Unless it's an emergency, we try to give one another at least a week's notice since the library has such a small staff."

"I understand." And I did. Besides, based on what I'd read about chikankari, even working around the clock, we wouldn't be able to put together a decent outfit with the time constraints we'd been given. Lowering my voice so Mom wouldn't hear, I added, "I don't know how we're going to pull this off. I mean, I have class tonight and tomorrow night. . . . and your taking a day off won't make much difference either way."

"Maybe we can use something I've already got," she said.

"Oh, hey, that could work. I'll see what Mom thinks about your idea. Thanks, Reggie."

After talking with Reggie, I ran her idea by Mom. "We're not trying to be slackers, of course; it's just that we didn't know we were going to have to pull this all together so soon. Plus, Vera and I aren't experienced in chikankari, and Reggie can't take today off. She's going to try to take tomorrow, but she's not sure she can."

"I know, darling. Everything will work out. We just need to stay positive, that's all. Using something Reggie already has might work wonderfully with just a bit of tweaking." As she bent and picked up Angus's tennis ball, I could almost hear that June Cleaver/fifties theme song music playing in my head.

She tossed the ball, and Angus chased it into the hallway.

"I'll get with Reggie sometime later today,"

Mom said, turning to me with a smile. "She might have the very garment we need hanging in her closet."

To be honest, I was concerned that Mom's cheery disposition was steeped in denial. I was afraid she was about to get a rude awakening. It came even sooner than I'd expected.

Before Vera could get to the shop so Mom could give us our instructions, Henry called. He needed for Mom to come out to the set right away and was sending Sonny over to get her.

"Duty calls," she said breezily.

"What do you want Vera and me to do until you get back?" I asked.

"Just work on the tunics you've started. Even if we don't use them now, we'll need them eventually."

Vera and I were working diligently on our tunics when Sadie came into the Seven-Year Stitch.

"I heard your movie crew is thinking of shooting some scenes near Ford's Mill," she said, as she petted Angus on the head.

I shrugged. "I don't know where Ford's Mill is. Reggie and I did take them to a spot on the outskirts of town where we had to pull off the road and hike up a steep hill, but I didn't see a mill."

"Then you didn't go far enough around the

hill." Sadie sat beside me on the sofa. "I'm sure the place you're talking about is Ford's Mill. Just tell your mom to have everybody be careful up there. The mill and outbuildings are dilapidated and about to fall down in some places, and some of the county people use it as everything from a homeless shelter to a landfill to a place to deal drugs."

"Oh, my," Vera said. "Paul will have to look into that. It might make a good investigative piece."

"Well, remember the gunman who shot at Ted?" I asked. "His body was found out there on the property, and a dirt biker nearly ran us over as we were hiking up the hill."

"A guy's body was found there, and the movie people are *still* interested in using the location?" Sadie asked.

I nodded. "Go figure. But, at least it will be secure. Since the property became a crime scene yesterday, the Tallulah County Police Department is posting a twenty-four-hour guard around the site."

"Still," Sadie said, "ask your mom to be careful."

"I will. She's pretty feisty, though. She knows how to take care of herself."

I had a full five minutes before I was forced to eat those words.

Mom called my cell phone. "Marcella, I'm at the Tallulah County Police Station."

"Why? What happened?"

"Babs was killed this morning," she said.

"What?!" I realized Vera and Sadie were gaping at me.

"I had nothing to do with it, but the police have brought me in for questioning," Mom said.

"What happened to her?" I asked.

"She fell. The police think she was pushed."

"But why are they interrogating you, Mom?"

"Because she and I had been arguing. Look, I'll tell you everything I know later," said Mom. "But could you please come to the station and give me a ride home?"

"Of course," I said. "I'll be right there."

I ended the call and, still openmouthed, returned my phone to the pocket of my jeans.

"What is it, dear?" Vera asked.

"It's Mom. . . . The Tallulah County Police Department is questioning her. Babushka Tru has apparently been murdered, and they must think Mom did it."

"She didn't, did she?" Sadie asked.

"Of course she didn't!" I was ninety-nine percent sure of that.

"You go on and see to Beverly," Vera said. "I'll watch the shop and Angus while you're gone." She was already taking her phone from her purse, and I knew she was bursting at the seams to fill Paul Samms in on this latest development.

"Do you need me to drive you?" Sadie asked.

"No, thanks. I appreciate the offer, but I'm fine."
I turned to Vera. "And thank you for keeping an
eye on Angus and the shop. I'll be back as quickly
as I can."

She waved me on as her call was answered.
"Hi, it's me. Have you heard about Babs Tru?"

As I hurried out the door, I hoped Vera wouldn't
include the bit about my mother being a suspect
as she relayed to Paul the scintillating news of
Babs' murder. But I knew it was bound to come
out sooner or later.

Chapter Seven

I was familiar with the location of the Tallulah County Police Department because I'd been questioned there myself after an elderly woman named Louisa Ralston had collapsed in the Seven-Year Stitch a few months earlier. Ms. Ralston had died, and her death had been ruled a homicide. Come to think of it, Mom had been questioned by the TCPD during their investigation into Ms. Ralston's death too. She'd been determined to exonerate me as a suspect in Ms. Ralston's homicide and had not endeared herself to the detectives in charge during that interrogation. As I swung the Jeep into the first available parking space, I hoped her attitude then wouldn't come back to bite her in the butt now.

I rushed inside where the dour-faced deputy-secretary sat behind a bulletproof-glass enclosure. She was chatting on the phone and turned away from the window. From her demeanor, I could tell she was on a personal call, and she'd turned her back to me while my mother was undergoing the Tallulah County Inquisition somewhere in the recesses of this building!

I banged my palm against the glass. She continued to ignore me.

I took my phone from my pocket, looked up the phone number, and called the Tallulah County Police Department. The deputy-secretary turned to put the first call on hold so she could take the incoming call.

"Tallulah County Police Department," she droned. "What is the nature of your call?"

"I need to speak with someone in charge so that I can report a rude secretary who's ignoring me while she takes a personal call."

Glaring at me, the deputy-secretary slammed down the receiver and buzzed me in. Before allowing me to proceed, she scanned my body with a metal-detecting wand and examined the contents of my purse. She then called someone to come and escort me before buzzing me through another door.

"Thank you," I said.

She merely aimed another baleful look in my direction before resuming her phone call.

When I stepped through the door, I was greeted by a familiar albeit not particularly friendly— face.

"Well, well, well, Ms. Singer, I guessed you'd be paying us a visit today."

"Your instincts are dead-on." I regretted using the phrase *dead on* to Detective Bailey as soon as I'd said it, given the circumstances; but once said, I couldn't very well reel the words back so I let them go, acting as if it wasn't awkward after all.

Warmer weather had made him trade the tweed sport jackets I'd previously seen him in for a lighter-weight navy jacket. His dark blond mustache still obscured his upper lip, though, and his bald spot reflected the overhead fluorescent lights as we walked down the hall.

"How's Detective Ray?" I asked, glancing at the framed photos of groups of officers that lined the hallway.

"Ask him yourself." Detective Bailey opened the door to an interrogation room.

Amid the sea of yellow and green plaid carpet, Mom sat at a gray metal table that had been bolted to the floor. I'd expected her to appear frightened or intimidated. Maybe it was some sort of projection of my own feelings because it was not a projection of hers.

"Detective Ray, would you be a dear and top off my coffee please?" she asked.

"Sure," he said. "Ms. Singer—Marcy—you can have ten minutes with your mother in the company of Detective Bailey and me."

I looked over at the square-bodied, gray-haired Detective Ray, and he raised his hand in a gesture that was not so much a wave as an acknowledgment of my presence. I nodded.

"I'll be right back." Detective Ray took Mom's coffee cup from the table. "Bailey?"

"Nah, I'm good."

I wasn't offered a beverage. I sat on the rust-cushioned metal chair across from Mom. "Are you okay? What happened?"

"I'm fine, darling. How are you? You look upset."

"Mom, I *am* upset. You're being questioned in a homicide investigation. This is not simply coffee and catching up with our buddies, Detectives Bailey and Ray."

"Oh, I know that," she said. "Although it *has* been delightful catching up with you." This comment was directed to Detective Bailey. "But don't get so jumpy, Marcella. I'm not the only one being questioned, and I've called Alfred. He's on his way."

Alfred Benton had been Mom's attorney for the past thirty years. My father had died when I was young, so Alfred had been a surrogate dad to me almost all my life.

"You heard that," I said to Detective Bailey. "Her attorney is on his way. You have no right to question her without her attorney being present."

"That's correct," he said. "We don't. Your mother chose to speak with us voluntarily."

I turned back to Mom. "Are you sure that's wise? Wouldn't you rather wait until Alfred gets here to give a statement?"

"Not really, darling. My statement is simple: I'm innocent. In fact, I'm not sure Babs' death was a murder at all. She might've just slipped and fell."

Detective Ray returned. He put Mom's coffee in front of her and then sat on the chair beside me.

"Mom, what happened?" I asked.

"Babs was messing around that old mill, and she fell," Mom said.

"Blunt-force trauma to the back of the victim's head combined with a possible murder weapon found at the crime scene indicate that the victim didn't fall but was knocked down through the hole to the floor eighteen feet below," Detective Bailey said.

"How do you know she didn't get the trauma when she fell?" Mom asked. "Falling eighteen feet is bound to have an adverse effect on one's body." She looked at me. "This is the issue the detectives and I keep going around and around on. We simply can't agree."

"Trust us," said Detective Ray. "We know that some of the victim's injuries occurred perimortem."

"How can you be sure of that?" I asked. "Has the autopsy been done?"

"No, but I saw the body myself," Detective Ray said. "When you've been in this business as long as I have, you know some things without having the benefit of the autopsy."

"Why do you think my mother had anything to do with Ms. Tru's death?"

"Like she said, we're talking with everybody," said Detective Ray. "But she was reportedly the last person to see the victim alive."

"And they were overheard having a heated argument," Detective Bailey added. He looked at his watch. "I'm afraid your time is up, Marcy. If you'd like to wait out in the hall, you may drive your mother back to Tallulah Falls when we're done talking with her."

I pushed back my chair. "Mom, would you like for me to call Riley Kendall?"

"No, thank you, darling. Alfred will be here tomorrow. Just let me finish up with Detectives Ray and Bailey, and I'll be right out."

I had to wonder if on the inside she was as nonchalant about this whole ordeal as she appeared to be on the outside.

A few minutes later, Mom stepped out of the interrogation room. I started to hug her, but she kept walking. I couldn't blame her. I was eager to put this place behind me too.

"Let us know if you plan to leave town, Ms. Singer," Detective Bailey said.

"I will," Mom and I said simultaneously.

I smiled uncomfortably and gave the officer a little wave before turning and following Mom down the hall.

We left the building and got into the Jeep. She remained stoic until I'd pulled out of the parking lot. Then she uttered a slight squeak and slumped in her seat.

I put on my signal light to move onto the shoulder of the road.

"Don't you dare stop here," Mom said. "I don't want them to see us and think I'm upset. Take me to your place."

"Okay." I turned the signal light off and accelerated. "What happened when you went to the set this morning?"

"Henry said Babs was aggravated with me because the initial costumes I'd made for her didn't fit properly." She huffed. "If you'd seen how that girl has been gorging herself at the hospitality table, you'd understand *why* the clothes I fitted her with last week will barely button now."

"So Henry called you over there to get new measurements?" I asked.

"Yes. So I went to the tent the crew has set up near an old mill. Ms. Hoity-Toity was in the tent waiting for me, attitude and all." Mom checked herself for a second. "I'm sorry to speak ill of the dead, and it's a tragedy she died so young. But that's just the way it happened. We had words."

"That would be where the *heated argument* overheard by witnesses comes in."

"Hey, she started it, not me," Mom said. "She insinuated that I'd measured her incorrectly the first time. She told me that if I'd known what I was doing to start with, we wouldn't be doing this again."

I pursed my lips. *Ouch.*

"I told *her* that if she'd ever met a cookie she could resist, we wouldn't be remeasuring," she said.

I winced. *Double ouch.*

"And that's when the argument got heated," Mom finished.

"I can imagine. Did the argument escalate into any slapping or hair-pulling . . . ?"

"Or blunt-force trauma? No, Marcella, it did not!"

"Oh, Mom, I know you didn't kill her. That's not what I meant. I'm just trying to get all the facts to help ensure you'll have a good defense."

"You *do* think I did it!"

"No, I don't," I insisted. "But if you end up getting charged with murder, you're going to need an excellent attorney to *prove* you didn't do it."

"I'm not being charged with anything. I didn't *do* anything."

"And how many movie scripts have you read where the heroine said the same thing and had a heck of a time proving it?"

She sighed. "Just take me home please. I'd like to lie down."

I dropped Mom off at home and returned to the Seven-Year Stitch. Vera was full of questions, as I'd expected her to be. Like Mom, I was worn out with the entire ordeal, so I merely told Vera that Tallulah County police detectives were questioning everyone to determine exactly what had happened to Ms. Tru.

"But they do believe Babs was murdered, don't they?" Vera asked.

"They won't know anything for certain until the autopsy has been done," I said. "The girl might've been exploring and just took a fall." Yeah, the thought of Babs Tru going off on an exploratory hike sounded hokey even to me, but I didn't want Vera's journalist boyfriend thinking— any more than he probably already did—that my mom had been accused of murder. So far, she had not been arrested, and I prayed she wouldn't be.

I thanked Vera for watching the shop and asked her to please excuse me while I called students and canceled the evening's classes.

"Of course, dear." Vera gave both Angus and me a quick hug. "Let me know if there's anything you or Beverly needs. I'm sure Paul would be more than glad to let her tell her side of the story."

"Thank you so much." I was proud to be able to say that without clenching my teeth. "I'll keep that in mind."

I blew out a breath as the door closed behind Vera and wondered where to begin. Relieved that, at the moment, there were no customers in the shop, I sat on one of the red club chairs and checked my phone. Ted had sent me a text message asking me to call him as soon as I could. I rang his phone.

"Hey, babe," he answered, his voice deep, slightly husky, and full of sympathy. "Are you okay? How's Bev?"

"We're all right. . . . Both of us are pretty shook up, though. She asked me to take her home, and I'm going to cancel this evening's classes so I can be there with her."

"That's good. If you'd like, I can bring dinner."

"A pizza with extra everything would be wonderful," I said. "I think we could use some comfort food."

"I'll also send a patrolman by every so often to make sure the media hounds don't camp out on your curb," Ted said. "Most of them will be swarming the movie set—they might already be there if word of Babushka Tru's death has hit the social media outlets yet—but there might be one or two that try to catch your mom once they find out where she's staying."

"Because she's the main suspect in the murder?" I asked.

"Right now the official word is that she and other members of the cast and crew are being called *persons of interest*. The TCPD doesn't want the media to jump to their own conclusions."

"There are bound to be leaks, though. Somebody is always looking for a chance to be the center of attention, settle a grudge, make a little money . . . something."

"Bev's gonna need a top-notch attorney," Ted said.

"Alfred is coming tomorrow," I said. "And that's a good start. But I'm afraid she's going to need someone with more criminal law experience."

"Yeah, she is. Remember Campbell Whitting, the guy who represented Calloway in the Graham Stott murder trial?"

"Of course. He was majorly impressive."

"Have Bev give him a call," he said.

"Do you think he'll take her on? When he agreed to take Todd's case, I gathered it was only because he was a friend of the family."

Ted barked out a mirthless chuckle. "A high-profile case like this is right up his alley, Marce. He'll put somebody on the back burner to sign on as your mom's counsel because he loves being in the spotlight doing what he does best."

Chapter Eight

At Mom's insistence, I didn't cancel my Tuesday evening class after all. I'd called and asked Ted to cancel the pizza since Mom insisted I carry on with life as usual.

I took Angus home for his dinner and realized that Mom had used cooking to try to get her mind off Babs' murder that afternoon. When I opened the front door, the delectable aromas made my mouth water. They apparently had a strong effect on Angus, too, because he sprinted to the kitchen. I, however, lingered in the foyer in an attempt to guess what dishes Mom had made. I could detect some type of beef . . . the yeasty, buttery scent of freshly baked bread . . . onions . . . potatoes, maybe? And something chocolate. Definitely, something chocolate.

"Hi, darling," Mom called from the kitchen. "I hope you don't mind—I made pot roast, and Ted's coming to eat with us."

"That's great, Mom," I said, kissing her cheek as I walked into the kitchen. "Thank you."

In addition to the pot roast—which included onions, carrots, and, yes, potatoes—Mom had made rolls and brownies.

"Is there anything I'm overlooking?" she asked. "Anything else you'd like?"

"No. You've outdone yourself as it is."

"Coffee," she said. "Ted might want coffee with his dessert. I'll make a pot of decaf."

As she busied herself with the coffeemaker, I started to tell her that wasn't necessary; but I realized it was. If she didn't occupy her thoughts with dinner and mundane things, she'd give in to the worry that she could actually be arrested for Babushka Tru's murder.

The doorbell rang, and Angus forgot his obsession with Mom and the dinner she'd prepared long enough to race to the entryway and bark. I trailed behind him and let Ted inside.

"Hey, buddy," Ted greeted Angus, as he pulled me to him for a quick kiss and hug. "How are you?"

"I'm fine."

"And Bev?" he asked softly.

"She's trying to avoid the situation as best as she can," I said. "She spent the afternoon cooking—I hope you like pot roast, by the way—and I'm pretty sure she won't be eager to talk about the murder."

"But we've *got* to talk about it."

"I know." I rested my head on his muscular chest. "Just don't jump right in with both feet. Give her time to warm up to the topic."

"I'll try," he promised. "Since she insisted on your keeping to your class schedule, we don't have a lot of time."

"I know." I blew out a breath before lifting my head. "Let's go."

Hand in hand, Ted and I walked into the kitchen.

"There you two are," Mom said brightly. "Ted, go ahead and have a seat. Marcella, I've almost finished setting the table, but I still need glasses."

"Gotcha."

"And cups and saucers so I can serve coffee with the dessert," she said.

"Wait, wait, wait," Ted said, with a grin. "Did I walk into Marcy's kitchen or some fancy five-star restaurant?"

"You might want to hold off on the exaggerated praise until after you've tasted the food," Mom said. "I seldom have occasion to cook anymore, so I'm out of practice."

Ted waited until Mom and I had finished setting the table and then pulled out our chairs in order to "seat us properly."

"Now *I* feel like the one in the fancy restaurant," Mom said.

We were a full five minutes into the meal before Ted broached the topic of Babushka Tru's murder. For him, that constituted not jumping in with both feet but merely tentatively testing the water with one toe *before* diving in.

"I know this is something you and Marcy are trying not to think about," he told Mom, "but you need to prepare yourself for the possibility that you could be arrested." He put down his fork and spread his hands. "I'm not saying that's going to happen, but we have to be ready if it does."

When the man dove, he dove in headfirst.

"Ted's right, Mom," I said, gently. "You need to tell us everything that happened today."

"I've already told you. Henry called and asked me to come to the set because Babs wasn't happy with the fit of her costumes," Mom said.

"That's good." Ted picked his fork back up and cut a chunk of potato in two. "You were summoned to the set by your employer. You didn't go and seek Babs out of your own volition."

I saw where he was going with that line of reasoning. Even if Mom was arrested, premeditation wouldn't be a factor. I knew Mom was innocent, and I didn't want her to be arrested at all; but if she was, it was good to know that first-degree murder would be off the table.

"I remeasured Babs in the portion of the mill that's serving as a makeshift wardrobe department, and then I went to gather up Babs' costumes and to talk with my assistants about letting them out."

"And did you talk with your assistants?" Ted asked.

Mom shook her head. "I couldn't find anyone. I sat down at a sewing station to begin the alterations myself, but it wasn't long before I heard a commotion. I went to see what had happened and learned that Babs had taken a fall and was dead."

"Detective Bailey said you'd been overheard arguing with Babs," I said.

"Yes, we argued. Babs and I clashed like pink stripes on a polka dot zebra and everyone knew it," Mom said. "So what?"

"So what is that it gives police a motive," I told her.

"What were you arguing about?" Ted asked.

"The initial measurements," Mom said. "Babs said I didn't do them correctly, and I insisted that she'd gained weight."

"Huh." Ted took a bite of his pot roast.

"Huh, what?" I asked.

He merely shrugged.

"Come on," I insisted. "That was a loaded *huh* if I've ever heard one."

Ted swallowed and wiped his mouth on his napkin. "It's just that your mom might've been right about Babs' weight gain."

"See? I told you how she was always stuffing her

face," Mom said. "Anyone could see she was plumping up."

I was still watching Ted. "That's not it, is it? What're you not saying?"

"One of the TCPD officers told me the medical examiner suspected that Babs might have been pregnant when she died."

I was still mulling over the shocking possibility that Babushka Tru might've been pregnant as I drove back to the shop for the candlewicking class. Angus had stayed home with Mom, and Ted had promised to send patrol cars by both my house and the Seven-Year Stitch every half hour to keep the media at bay. He'd also said he'd come to the shop after class to see me home. I protested that all his precautions were unnecessary, but I was really touched that he cared so much.

As I took my candlewick embroidery work-in-progress out of my tote bag and placed it on the coffee table in the sit-and-stitch square, I remembered Ron Fitzpatrick telling me that it was widely believed that Henry Beaumont had been having an affair with Babs. If it was true that Babs had been pregnant, was Henry the baby's father? Mom had dismissed the gossip about Babs and Henry, but she'd said herself time and time again that emotions run amok in the movie world. Everyone was driven by something: a desire to be loved, a need for acceptance, a hunger for money and fame, a fear of growing old and fading into oblivion. And when a beautiful young woman desperate for renewed Hollywood success crossed paths with a famous producer-director who just might be starting to worry about his age and his virility . . . well, anything was possible . . . even if that producer-director was a married man.

I checked the mini-fridge in my office to make sure it was well stocked with bottled water. Then I put an assortment of hard candies in a glass bowl and placed it in the center of the coffee table.

I looked up when the bells over the shop door jingled. I was expecting to see the first of my students arriving, not a Tallulah County Police Department deputy.

My heart fluttered up into my throat, and I sounded hoarse as I asked, "May I help you?"

The uniformed officer was wearing an eight-point cap, which he removed and held in front of him as he stood with his chest out and his feet shoulder-width apart like a soldier. "Yes. I understand Beverly Singer is your mother and that she's staying with you for the duration of her visit to Tallulah Falls."

My mouth went so dry that my voice emerged as a croak. "Is she okay?"

"Oh, yes, ma'am. I'm so sorry." He stepped forward and steadied me with his strong right hand as I sank onto the sofa facing the window. "I didn't consider that you might interpret my question as an indication something had happened to her."

I merely stared at him.

"Gee, I do apologize," he said after a moment. "You've turned as pale as a ghost. May I get you something?"

I shook my head. "Why are you here?"

"Oh, yeah." He chuckled slightly. "My bad. I—we, that is—I mean, the captain . . . and of course, I think it's a good idea too . . . we thought you should know that we believe you need to hire some extra security . . . you know, like a bodyguard or something."

At some point during—I checked the nameplate—Deputy Preston's convoluted explanation for his presence in my shop, my mouth dropped open. I thought to close it after asking, "Why do you feel that way?"

"Well, there's a bunch of reporters and stuff already swarming the movie set," said Deputy Preston. "They're kind of a wily group. It won't take long for them to realize you're Beverly Singer's daughter, and then they'll be beating down your doors . . . here and at home."

Being a county deputy instead of a townie, he was apparently unaware that I was dating a "bodyguard" and that I had a four-legged one on standby as well.

"I appreciate your concern." I nodded toward the sidewalk where some of my students were approaching. "But if you'll excuse me, I have a class getting ready to start."

"Oh, sure." He removed a business card from the breast pocket of his shirt and handed it to me. "If you need anything, just give me a call, all right?"

"Will do," I said with a stiff smile. I read the card as I got up and went to the office to get a bottle of water. *Deputy Robert Preston.* Mom would get a kick out of the irony of the kid's name being the same as that of a Hollywood legend.

Sadie was one of the first students in the shop. Normally, Sadie is as far removed from an embroidery enthusiast as one can get, other than to *ooh* and *ahh* over things other people have made. She'd signed up for the candlewicking class because it was a fairly simple beginner's class and because we'd had a bit of a tiff just before the class commenced and signing up had been her version of extending an olive branch.

"Marce, may I speak with you privately for a sec before class gets started?" she asked.

"Sure." I ushered her into my office and pushed up the door. "What's going on?"

"I wanted to warn you that MacKenzies' Mochas' customers have been asking questions about your mom and you all afternoon," she said. "Todd told Blake that he and his staff at the Brew Crew have been dodging a lot of Nosy Nellies themselves."

"Are they reporters?" I asked.

"Some are. Others are simply curious about the murder, especially since it happened to a celebrity."

I rubbed my forehead. "It hasn't even officially been ruled a homicide yet."

"As far as these people are concerned, it has," Sadie said. "Just be leery of them."

"One of the Tallulah County deputies came by right before you got here and said pretty much the same thing. He advised me to hire some extra security." I scoffed. "*Extra*, like I have bodyguards surrounding me wherever I go."

"Well, if you count Angus and Ted. . . ." She grinned. "But, seriously, hon, you might want to give it some thought for you *and* your mom. Some of these *inquiring-mind* types can be awfully pushy."

"I'll talk with Mom and Ted and see what they think." I opened the door, and Sadie and I joined the rest of the students.

Most of them were regulars—meaning, they joined at least one class a session: Vera, Reggie, Julie, and her daughter Amber. It was Amber who brought up the subject of Babushka Tru after we'd all got settled in and were working on our projects.

"Did you guys hear about BTru getting killed?" she asked. "It apparently happened somewhere near here."

"Be true?" Reggie asked with a frown.

"Yeah," Amber said. "That's what the magazines in the grocery store call her—BTru. You know, like JLo for Jennifer Lopez or Biebs for Justin Bieber? Her real name is Babushka Trublonski—they shortened the last name to Tru."

No wonder. Babushka Trublonski was a mouthful. Funny, but I'd never heard anyone mention Babs' real last name before. Amber must be quite a fan.

"I'd forgotten the tabloids called her BTru," Vera said. "I'll be sure to remind Paul of that. He might want to reference it."

While I was under the impression that any reporter worth his salt wouldn't have to be reminded of such things because he'd thoroughly research his subject before writing about her, I held my tongue. I needed to stay out of this conversation, if at all possible.

"I'm amazed at how quickly the media has begun storming our little town," Sadie said. "I mean, she died only this morning."

"It's already being reported on TMZ and E!," Amber said.

"You watch too much of that junk," her mother admonished.

"Are they calling the death an accident or a homicide?" Vera asked Amber.

Amber shrugged. "They said she fell to her death on the set of her new movie. Why? Did you hear she was pushed or something?"

"At this point, anything and everything said by the media and the public is mere speculation," Reggie said. "No one knows for sure what happened."

"How's everyone doing on their project?" I asked. I leaned closer to an elderly lady who'd been working steadily and hadn't even looked up during the Babushka Tru discussion. "Muriel, are you doing okay?"

Muriel raised her cottony head and smiled. "I'm fine, thanks. How are you, dear?"

I was getting ready to reply to Muriel that I too was fine when the bells over the shop door jingled. A woman in a black coat with a leopard-print collar was standing just inside the door. She staggered slightly as she tottered in black stiletto boots toward the sit-and-stitch square, and I quickly put down my embroidery to meet her halfway.

"Hi, I'm Marcy Singer. May I help you?"

"I hope so. I'm Mita Trublonski—Babs' mother."

Chapter Nine

I could feel the eyes of the students burning into my back. I didn't dare turn and face their curiosity outright. Instead, I asked Mita Trublonski—Babushka Tru's mother, yikes!—to step into my office. I called over my shoulder to the students that I'd be back in just a moment.

I settled Ms. Trublonski into my desk chair and gave her a bottle of water. "I'm terribly sorry for your loss."

Ms. Trublonski uncapped the bottle and drank deeply. "Thank you."

"I'm not sure how I can help you," I said.

"I understand that your mother is Beverly Singer and that she was one of the last people to see my Babs alive." With trembling hands, she replaced the cap on the water bottle. "I'd like to talk with your mother . . . and anyone else who might've been with Babs that morning."

"Of course," I said. "If you'll excuse me for a second, I'll make sure this is a good time for her." I slipped out of the office and down the hall to the bathroom to call Mom.

"You'll never guess who's in my office right now," I said when Mom answered the phone.

"Oliver Stone? Tim Burton? Peter Jackson? Peter Pumpkin-Eater?" she asked.

"Mom, this is serious. Have you been drinking?"

"Of course not. I'm just trying to lighten the mood and pretend my life isn't hanging in the balance here."

"Oh . . . yeah . . . well. . . ." I felt bad for asking if she'd been drinking. But it was obvious that Babs' mom had been. And under the circumstances, I'd probably at least consider it.

"So, who's in your office?" Mom asked.

"Um, Babs' mother—Mita Trublonski. Do you know her?"

"I've seen her on set a time or two, but I've never actually met her. What does she want?"

"To talk with you," I said.

"Why? Does she think I killed her daughter? Is she crazy?"

"I don't think so. She seems drunk—or, at least, a little tipsy—but she isn't raging around slinging accusations against anyone." I peeped out the door and spotted Ms. Trublonski in the hall. Oh, no! She was headed back into the shop! I didn't want her talking with the students without me there.

"If you want to talk with her, I'll see if Ted can bring her," I continued. "That'll keep her off the road and give you some protection in case she *is* nutty or something." I took another look out the door and saw that Ms. Trublonski was nearly to the sit-and-stitch square. "Mom, I need to go. What do you want to do?"

"I'll talk with the woman," Mom said. "I feel I owe her that."

"Okay. See you soon."

As I hurried down the hall, I texted Ted and asked him if he could come by the shop, pick up Babushka Tru's mother, and drive her to my house. I told him that if so, I'd explain everything better when he got to the Seven-Year Stitch.

I got to the sit-and-stitch square and explained to Mita that Ted would be by to take her to see my mother. She nodded and tottered into one of the red club chairs.

"You have a lovely shop," she told me.

"Thank you," I said.

She waved her well-manicured hand toward my slack-jawed students. "Please don't let me interrupt you. Go back to your sewing."

As I reclaimed my seat on the sofa beside Muriel, my phone buzzed. I casually took it from my pocket, glanced at the screen, and read Ted's text:

On my way. I stifled my sigh of relief as I slid the phone back into my jeans pocket.

Most of the candlewicking students were looking anywhere other than at Mita Trublonski. Reggie and Sadie were staring at but not working on their projects. Vera was looking at me and raising her eyebrows as if she and I could somehow communicate using some sort of facial Morse code. And Julie was not-so-subtly nudging her daughter, who was gazing openmouthed at our guest.

I was trying to come up with a way to break the uncomfortable silence when Amber beat me to the punch.

"Ms. Trublonski, your daughter was so awesome," she said. "She was like my favorite actress of all time."

"Thank you." Ms. Trublonski smiled sadly. "On the one hand, it's hard to believe she's gone. But on the other hand, the poor darling had been a train wreck for years. I suppose you keep up with the tabloids and know she'd been arrested for DUI and drug possession more than once. She'd gone to court-mandated rehab twice."

"But this time it took," Amber said, seemingly oblivious to Julie's death grip on her forearm. "I know it did. She'd just been under so much pressure since *Surf Dad* was canceled, that's all. This movie was going to be her comeback. She was gonna be on top again. She was gonna be great."

"You're very sweet," Ms. Trublonski said. "I appreciate your kind words. And you're absolutely right about the pressure Babs had been under. The tabloids speak as if they know everything, but they don't. They didn't know the half of what Babs had been through."

By that point, everyone except Muriel, who was still plugging away at her embroidery, was hanging on Ms. Trublonski's words.

"*Surf Dad* was Babushka's life for five years," Ms. Trublonski continued. "The other people who'd worked on the show were like extended family to her. She believed they'd all keep in touch after the show was canceled." She sighed. "The child was eleven when it ended. What was she supposed to think?"

"I read that it broke her heart when Andrew Mains asked Sabrina Willis to play his daughter in that race car movie," Amber said.

"Amber, you need to be quiet and work on your pillow," Julie said.

"No, that's all right," Ms. Trublonski said. "I don't mind talking about Babs." She looked at Amber. "That *did* break her heart. After playing Andrew's daughter on *Surf Dad* for five seasons, Babs thought she was a shoo-in for the role. But he—and the studio—chose Sabrina. They said that if they'd gone with Babs, it would have made the movie seem like too much of an extension of *Surf Dad*."

I agreed that it would have, but I wisely held my tongue on the subject.

"Well, after getting that slap in the face, didn't Babs' boyfriend take up with that snotty little Sabrina too?" Vera leaned forward, her demeanor more that of a teenager than Amber's.

"Lane Peck dated Sabrina for a short time, but I wouldn't say he'd ever been Babs' boyfriend," Ms. Trublonski said. "That so-called romance was primarily the invention of Lane's manager and tabloid speculators when they were costars. Babs preferred guys older than her . . . sometimes much older. I think she was always searching for someone to replace her father."

My mind instantly flew to Henry Beaumont. Had he been Babs' latest father-figure boyfriend? Or was that, too, merely speculation?

"Is Babs' father dead?" Vera asked.

Mita Trublonski shook her head. "No, but he might as well be, as far as Babushka was concerned. During her third season of *Surf Dad*, he embezzled a sizable chunk of her income and then took off with his secretary." She uncapped the water bottle, took a drink, and then slumped against the back of the chair. She suddenly appeared tired and sad.

I was relieved when Ted arrived. I met him at the door and gave him a quick, whispered rundown of the situation.

"I'm pretty sure she's been drinking," I said. "That's one reason I don't want her driving over to see Mom by herself."

"And the other reason is obvious," he said. "From the look of things, your class has come to a standstill. Why don't you close up shop and come with us?"

"Mainly because I don't want half the class showing up at my house."

He nodded. "Vera looks as if she might come anyway."

"She might. She eats celebrity gossip up like a bear eats a salmon." I raised my voice as Ted and I approached the sit-and-stitch square. "Ms. Trublonski, this is Ted Nash. As I said, he's going to drive you over to my house so you can talk with Mom."

Ms. Trublonski started to get up but lost her balance and fell back onto the chair. On her second attempt, she stood. "I'll follow you in my car."

"No, please, allow me to be your Tallulah Falls tour guide." Ted gave her his most charming smile and offered her his arm.

She took his arm and looked grateful for the support. "Well, I am a little unsteady this evening. Are you sure you don't mind?"

"I'm positive." He nodded at me. "Marcy, we'll see you as soon as class is over."

"I'll be there as quickly as I can." I gave him a quick kiss on the cheek.

The shop was unusually quiet as Ted and Mita Trublonski left. Abandoning all pretense of being able to concentrate on my candlewicking project, I sat on the club chair Ms. Trublonski had vacated. Everyone was staring at me as if waiting for me to speak. Everyone except Muriel, that is, who continued to make Colonial knots, content in her own little world. At that moment, I envied Muriel that serenity.

When I didn't say anything, Vera jumped in. "What does she want to talk with your mom about? Does she think Beverly had anything to do with Babs' death?"

"I don't know," I said. "She didn't appear antagonistic. I think maybe she's simply reaching out to the people who saw her daughter before she died. Babs is gone. I believe the poor woman is scrambling for any last crumb of the girl's existence . . . anything she can cling to."

When I arrived at my house, the porch light was on, and Ted's car was in the driveway. I noticed extra vehicles lining both sides of the street, but that fact and its importance didn't really register until later.

As I got out of the Jeep, Angus jumped up and

placed his front paws on the fence. He barked a friendly greeting, and I told him I'd bring him inside soon. Mom had apparently put him into the backyard for Mita Trublonski's comfort.

Other than Angus barking and a few frogs chirping, the neighborhood was deceptively quiet. I walked into the house and put my purse and keys on the table in the entryway. I heard voices coming from the kitchen.

"Hi," I said upon entering the kitchen and taking the only vacant chair. Mom was to my left, Mita Trublonski was directly across from me, and Ted was to my right. I briefly examined each of their faces, but their expressions weren't giving anything away.

They returned my greeting, and then Mom offered me some coffee.

"No, thanks, I'm good."

Ms. Trublonski pushed her chair back from the table. "Thank you so much for taking the time to meet with me, Beverly, but I really must be going."

What? I'd only just got here, and the woman was *leaving*?

"Please don't hurry off on my account," I said with a smile.

"Oh, not at all, dear," Ms. Trublonski said. "It's been a long, hard day, and I'd like to go to my hotel and lie down now."

"Of course," I said. I was disappointed, but I knew Mom would give me the play-by-play as soon as Ms. Trublonski left.

Ted stood. "I'll take you back to your car. Or, if you're too tired to drive, I can take you directly to your hotel. It's whatever you prefer."

"Drop me at my car please," she said. "I can make it the rest of the way."

Ted told me he'd be back soon, and Ms. Trublonski thanked us all again for our hospitality as we walked her to the door. As soon as Ted opened the door, though, our congenial scene turned chaotic. Flashbulbs went off, Angus barked furiously, and reporters yelled questions.

"Ms. Trublonski, do you believe your daughter was murdered?"

"Do you think Beverly Singer had anything to do with your daughter's death?"

"Beverly, did Babs' mother come here to confront you with killing her daughter?"

"Is it true that Babs was pregnant when she died?"

Ted pulled Ms. Trublonski back inside and closed the door. "I'll take care of this." He turned to me. "Have you got a blanket or cape or something Ms. Trublonski can borrow to shield her from the cameramen?"

"Sure." I hurried to the living room, went to the closet, and took out a green flannel throw.

I returned to the entryway as Ted stepped out onto the porch with his badge raised and pulled the door up behind him.

"I'm Detective Ted Nash of the Tallulah Falls Sheriff's Department," he called. "You're on private property and will be arrested for trespassing if you don't get off this lawn immediately. Neither Ms. Trublonski nor Ms. Singer has any desire to speak with any of you. Should you attempt to approach either of them, you will be arrested for harassment."

Ted came back inside. "Are you ready to go, Ms. Trublonski?"

"Yes." She took the blanket I offered her and draped it over her head. "Thank you."

When Ted opened the door again, the yard had been cleared of reporters. The flashbulbs still clicked, though, and Angus continued his fervent protests. I closed the door and locked it, but Mom and I watched from behind the curtains at the picture window in the living room to make sure Ted and Ms. Trublonski were able to make an undisturbed exit.

As soon as they'd backed out of the driveway, I ran to the kitchen door to let Angus in. I was relocking the door when Mom joined me in the kitchen.

"Are you okay?" I asked.

She nodded and sat down at the table. Angus went to lie by her feet. She sighed, and so did he.

I decided I needed a cup of coffee after all. "Is this decaf?"

Again, Mom nodded.

I poured myself a cup and added cream and artificial sweetener. "Want me to top off your cup?"

"No, thanks."

I was relieved that she'd found her voice again. I sat down beside her and took her hand. "It'll be all right. We'll get through this."

I was nearly bursting to ask her what Ms. Trublonski had said to her, but I could tell this wasn't the time to ask. If she wanted to talk about it, she would. If not, I wouldn't press her. I'd simply wait and ask Ted.

I held her hand, sipped my coffee, and finally she spoke.

"She came to ask me if I thought Babs had committed suicide."

"What? What did you say?"

"I told her what I believe is the truth. Although I didn't know Babs that well, I feel her death was a tragic accident."

"Had Ms. Trublonski been told that it . . . . you know . . . that her death seemed . . . suspicious?" I asked.

"She knows it's rumored that Babs was murdered, but she thinks the rumor is simply a tool to continue to exploit Babs in death," Mom said.

"You know there's more to it than that."

She shrugged. "Maybe she's right. Think of how many magazine articles and televised stories could be sold about the unsolved murder of a young Hollywood starlet."

"Is that what you truly believe?"

"I'm not sure what I believe at this point," she said.

Chapter Ten

By the time Ted returned from seeing Mita Trublonski safely to her car, Mom had already gone upstairs to bed. I knew she was exhausted, but I also thought she wanted to be alone more than anything. During the crises of others, Mom was terrific. She could remain positive, upbeat, and strong—a rock for those around her to lean on. But her personal crises—like when Dad died— drove her into a shell. She wanted to close herself off from everyone physically and emotionally un- til the crisis had either passed or enough time had elapsed to allow her to come to grips with the new normal left in the wake of the crisis.

I understood the behavior, but it was hard to ac- cept. I wanted to help her. I wanted to fix things for her. But I realized that in some ways this latest crisis was even harder for Mom to navigate than when Dad died. Then she had a child she had to care for, so she threw herself into looking after me and doing her work. Babushka Tru's death could destroy the career Mom had worked so hard to build . . . and that was even if Mom *wasn't* arrested and charged with murder. The stigma alone could ruin her.

I was sitting in the living room and heard Ted's car pull into the driveway. I hurried to the front door to greet him and was relieved to see that most of the media had gone.

"I only hope this isn't the quiet before the storm," I told Ted. "I've never had to deal with reporters much, and I don't like it. Even though Mom has worked on some high-profile movies, the press junkets occur post-production and then typically involve only the stars and other major players like the producers and directors."

We moved back into the living room and sat on the sofa. Ted pulled me to him, and I rested my head against his chest, soothed by his rhythmic heartbeat. I loved being in his arms.

"I wouldn't be surprised if there are several back here on your street tomorrow morning . . . although most of them are camped out near Mita Trublonski's hotel now," Ted said.

"A lot of the media attention focused on Mom depends on what the police learn—and reveal— within the next day or so, doesn't it?" I asked.

"That and whatever is leaked by anonymous sources. There's widespread speculation and quite a bit of money being offered, I imagine. That can be a dangerous combination in the hands of tabloids."

"Yes, it can. Mom told me about Mita Trublonski's fear that Babs had committed suicide," I said. "Will the police take that possibility into consideration as they continue their investigation?"

"They will, but I doubt Ms. Trublonski's fear would be enough to get them to change their minds about Babs' death being a homicide. From what I've gathered, preliminary findings at the crime scene indicated that Babs was struck on the back of the head with a blunt object prior to her fall."

"So it's only a matter of whodunit," I said.

"Yeah." Not knowing what else to say, Ted simply held me tighter.

That was exactly what I needed. We sat like that—quiet, comfortable, and contemplative—until my phone rang. It was Henry Beaumont.

"Marcy, I'm trying to reach Bev, but my calls just go to voice mail. Is she with you?"

"I'm afraid she's already gone to bed," I told him. "I can wake her if it's important."

"No," he said. "Don't bother her. I just need to talk with her about what she saw this morning. I've left her a couple messages, but please ask her to call me first thing tomorrow."

"I will, Henry."

"Thanks, dear. I—" He blew out a breath. "Never mind. Just have her call me."

When I ended the call, I placed my phone on the end table and cuddled back up to Ted. "That was the producer-director. Do you think I should wake Mom and have her call him back?"

"No. In the first place, she needs her rest," he said. "In the second place, she needs to speak with her attorneys before she talks with anyone else . . . especially another suspect."

I groaned. "I want this nightmare to be over. One of the Tallulah County Police Department deputies even came to the shop before class this evening and suggested I hire extra security. *Extra.* Like the team of heavily armed bodyguards I already employ isn't enough."

"Ha, ha. I'll try to have the regular patrol officers do an extra check both here and at the Stitch. But don't hesitate to call nine-one-one if anyone harasses you."

"Okay. Thanks." I kissed him.

"You're welcome. I might patrol myself if that's how you show your appreciation."

"Come by anytime."

Our next kiss was interrupted by my phone ringing again. I glanced at it and saw that it was Vera. I let the call go to voice mail.

"What am I going to tell her tomorrow?" I wondered aloud. "I know she'll want all the gory details of what Ms. Trublonski had to say to Mom."

"Tell her the truth. As soon as you got here, Ms. Trublonski left. You didn't hear a thing."

"Oh, you're good."

He chuckled. "Isn't that what happened?"

"Yeah . . . but you spin it so well," I said. "Not to change the subject, but the thought of spinning made me think of the dirt biker who nearly ran down Reggie, Sonny, Ron and me yesterday. Did the Tallulah County Police Department catch that guy?"

"No. They're looking for the bike and a person matching the description of the driver, but the bike has probably been hidden, and there's not much to go on with regard to the driver."

"That's true. He . . . or she . . . popped up over that hill so quickly, we only had time to react."

"The TCPD is fairly certain the biker was working with the gunman we'd been chasing," said Ted. "While they haven't found evidence to substantiate it yet, they think it's a pretty safe bet that the biker shot our gunman to death."

"Has the gunman been identified yet?"

"Yeah. His wallet with photo identification was in the back pocket of his jeans. He was a student at Tallulah County Junior College. He was studying computer science."

"Was he a hacker?" I asked. "Is that why he was stealing smartphones and computers?"

Ted nodded. "It's sad. The kid had his whole

life ahead of him, and that's what he chose to do with it?"

"We're getting way too depressed here," I said. "We need to lighten the mood . . . try not to think about murder and mayhem for a few minutes. Where were we before Vera called and interrupted us?" I caressed his face as I drew his mouth to mine. "Did I mention that Angus went to bed with Mom?"

Alfred Benton, Mom's attorney for as long as I could remember, and Campbell Whitting arrived before nine o'clock the next morning. I greeted Alfred with a hug and a kiss on the cheek.

"I'm glad you're here," I said to him quietly. "Mom's beginning to withdraw more and more."

Alfred was a tall, thin man with a full head of white hair that he kept neatly trimmed in a military-style cut. His very presence was one of imposing elegance. Should you have found him on the opposite side of the table from you in a legal battle, you should have been concerned . . . on the same side—relieved.

"We'll take care of this," Alfred said. "Marcy, have you met Campbell Whitting?"

"Not personally, but I know he did a fantastic job representing my friend Todd Calloway earlier this year," I said.

Mr. Whitting stepped around Alfred to take my

outstretched hand and give it a firm shake. He was a masterful man with bushy gray hair and a beard to match.

"Ah, yes," he said. "Todd is a good man. I'm glad I was able to help him out." There was a twinkle in his hazel eyes that belied the steel I'd seen Mr. Whitting display in the courtroom.

"Cam is the best criminal defense attorney on the West Coast," Alfred said. "He'll get your mother out of this mess."

"I know," I said. "Come on into the kitchen."

As I led the way, Alfred asked about Angus.

"He's playing in the backyard at the moment," I said. "It's always good to let him get some exercise before we head to the Seven-Year Stitch." I explained to Mr. Whitting that the Seven-Year Stitch was my embroidery specialty shop.

"I've seen it," he said. "It's right across the street from Todd's pub."

"That's right." I smiled. "Would either of you care for a cup of coffee?"

Mr. Whitting declined, but Alfred accepted a cup with two sugars. I was just about to call Mom to come downstairs when she entered the kitchen.

She was elegantly dressed in a peach silk pantsuit with a white lace camisole, but her pallor and the dark under-eye circles that showed through despite the carefully applied makeup indicated she'd rested very little if at all last night.

"Good morning." She greeted Alfred with a restrained hug and Campbell Whitting with a handshake. "I hope the two of you haven't been waiting long." She shot an admonishing glare in my direction.

"They just got here."

"We only arrived seconds ago."

The fact that Alfred and I had spoken simultaneously made us share a conspiratorial grin. I set his coffee on the table and then squeezed his arm affectionately.

"Mom, would you like some coffee?" I asked.

"No, thank you." She sat down at the table and motioned for the men to join her. They sat, and I started to do so as well. "Marcella, would you give us some privacy please?"

I drew in my breath. She was asking *me*—the one person in this room who'd been in a similar situation—to leave? My eyes darted from Mom's to Alfred's.

He gave me an almost imperceptible nod. "Would it be all right for me to stop by the Seven-Year Stitch later? I'd love to see the place."

"That would be great," I said. "Since Angus and I aren't needed here, I suppose we'll see you later in town then."

"I'll look forward to it," Alfred said.

When we got to the shop, I put Angus inside, relocked the door, and then stomped on down the street to MacKenzies' Mochas. I'd planned on having coffee at home with the grown-ups, but noooo. I'd been sent to my room—or, in this case, to the Seven-Year Stitch. *Run along like a good little girl, Marcella. The adults have business to discuss.*

I flung open the door, walked to the bar—the coffeehouse had been a bar before Blake and Sadie converted it—and flopped onto a stool.

Although Blake was usually the one who manned the bar, this morning it was Sadie. "Ooh." She grimaced. "What's wrong?"

"Who knows? Mom's attorneys came to talk with her and she asked me to give them some privacy. Can you believe that?"

"That is tough," she said. "The usual?"

I nodded. "Thanks." I stared down at the gleaming wood grain, tracing a dark line with my fingertip. "It's just so darn insulting, you know? I'm an adult. I want to know what's going on. I *deserve* to know what's going on."

Sadie put my low-fat vanilla latte with cinnamon on the bar and pushed it gently toward me. "You know all those times in the past when I asked you if you'd called your mom yet to ask about this or that, and you told me no because you didn't want to worry her? Like the time someone knocked you out in the alley and—"

"This is entirely different," I interrupted. "She

wasn't here when that happened. There was nothing she could do."

"Maybe there's nothing you can do now." She glanced around to make sure we weren't being overheard. "Maybe her attorneys are the only ones who can help her, and she doesn't want you getting all upset or something."

My eyes widened. "Wait a second. You don't think. . . ." I, too, made sure no one was listening and then lowered my voice to a hiss. "You don't think she did it, do you? What kind of crap have those tabloid jerks been spreading?"

"I didn't say I believe she did anything wrong," Sadie said. "I said maybe the attorneys are the only ones she wants to tell everything she knows . . . everything that happened on that hill yesterday morning." She looked around again before taking a cloth from the pocket of her apron and wiping the bar. "Only she knows what she saw, Marce. Maybe she's trying to protect you."

"I don't know what she's doing," I said. "I only know that I don't like being left out." I got up, put my money on the bar, and swiped up my latte. "Thanks again. I'll talk with you later."

I stepped back out onto the street and nearly ran headlong into the police officer who'd visited my shop yesterday before class.

"Oh, I'm so sorry, Deputy Preston. I wasn't watching where I was going."

"It's my fault," he said, with a laugh. "I'm paid to serve and protect, remember?"

"Yeah, but it's hard to protect against clumsiness."

"You seem to have a lot on your mind this morning. Is everything all right?" Deputy Preston asked.

I started to speak but waited until a couple walking past had gone on into the coffee shop.

"Yes," I said. "Everything's fine."

"Okay. See you later then." He grinned and nodded before going into MacKenzies' Mochas.

I went on up the street to the Seven-Year Stitch and reopened the shop. Angus, as receptive as ever to my moods, greeted me calmly. When I sank onto the red club chair, he sat beside me and placed his head on my lap. I stroked his fur and wondered about what Sadie had said. Had Mom seen something yesterday that she didn't want me to know about? Had she seen who'd really killed Babushka Tru? Maybe I wasn't the only person she was protecting.

I started when the bells over the shop door jingled. Angus spun around, and began barking as he charged our visitor.

"Whoa, there, big fella!" Deputy Preston, a coffee in one hand, raised his free hand and laughed. "I guess you do have some protection after all, Ms. Singer."

"Angus, it's all right. Come back here."

Angus did as I asked and returned to my side, only slightly "woofing" one last time.

"I'm sorry," I told Deputy Preston. "You startled me, and he reacted to that. He usually loves having company."

"Seems like you're in a bit of a fog this morning," he said. "That's why I came back to check on you after seeing you on the street. I wanted to make sure you're okay."

I smiled. "I'm fine, thanks. I do appreciate your concern. And you weren't kidding about those media hounds, were you? We had plenty of those last night. They reminded me of vultures sitting on a fence post in the desert . . . just waiting."

"Oh, they're vultures, all right." He shook his head. "Some are nice enough, I guess, just doing their jobs, you know. But others are not only intrusive, but mean-spirited."

"Do you have a minute?" I asked, gesturing toward the sofa.

"Sure." He glanced at his watch. "I have about ten of them actually."

"I know you aren't at liberty to discuss an ongoing investigation," I said. "But my Mom isn't saying much about what happened yesterday. Is there *anything* you can tell me?"

He rubbed the lower part of his face with his free hand. "I shouldn't. I really shouldn't say a word." He looked at me; then his eyes darted around the shop, and then back at me. "You promise you won't say anything?"

"I won't say a word."

"Not a word? I'd get fired if my captain knew I was telling you this," he said.

"Not one word," I said.

He sipped his coffee. "I really shouldn't."

I waited, knowing he was obviously dying to tell me whatever it was he *shouldn't* tell me.

He took a deep breath and then spit his words out quickly. "I heard them fighting—your mom and Babs. Babs was telling her that Henry would ruin her if she didn't do things her—Babs'—way. Your mom said she'd never kowtow to some still-wet-behind-the-ears diva, and that she didn't know why Henry put up with her. Babs told her to ask Henry which one of them he preferred, and then somebody slapped somebody."

"You mean, the fight actually got physical?"

"Yeah. I was starting to intervene when I saw Babs run past the window. Your mom went after her." Deputy Preston took another sip of his coffee. "A few minutes later, Ms. Singer left. I know your mom didn't mean to do anything, but it really doesn't look good for her at this point."

"You think my mother actually killed Babushka Tru?" I asked.

"I didn't say that."

Chapter Eleven

I desperately wanted to talk with Ted but didn't want to disturb him at work, so I texted him as soon as Deputy Preston left. I'd told the deputy I wouldn't *say* anything to anyone. I didn't say I wouldn't text it. Besides, I could trust Ted not to betray Deputy Preston to his superiors. I told Ted about the argument the deputy said escalated into a physical altercation between Mom and Babs.

"He seems to think Mom might've accidentally killed Babs," I texted.

To my relief, Ted called me back within minutes.

"Babe, everyone at the Tallulah County Police Department has a theory about what happened to Babs, and everyone in the media does too. Try not to be too concerned . . . at least, not yet. It's all just conjecture."

"But she ran me off this morning," I said. "She

asked me to give her, Alfred, and Cam Whitting some privacy."

"I think she's trying to keep you from worrying."

"And not knowing helps in what way?"

He laughed softly. "Talk with her about it then. Ask her why she didn't want you at their meeting."

"Did she say anything to you and Mita Trublonski last night that would indicate she knows more than she's telling?" I asked.

"Everyone always knows more than they're telling. That's human nature," he said. "I've got to run, but I'll be there at lunch, and I'll bring comfort food. We'll figure this out."

"Thanks." I felt better after talking with Ted. If anyone could help me sort this mess out, it was him.

An attractive woman in a coral business suit came into the shop. Her hair was in a French twist, and she wore pearl earrings. She smiled at me and said, "Good morning," before I even had a chance to welcome her to the Seven-Year Stitch.

"How may I help you?" I asked.

"I'm looking for a few . . . embroidery . . . things," she said. "I'll need some thread, and needles, and probably a piece of fabric."

Uh-huh. "How about a frame or a hoop? Do you need either of those?"

Angus bounded over to greet her.

"What a pretty dog! I don't think I need either of those things you mentioned. I'm making this into a pillow rather than framing it or . . . hooping it."

"Which do you generally prefer—hoops or frames?" I asked.

Her eyes darted left, then right. "I don't know. Which do *you* prefer?"

"You don't really embroider, do you?"

"This is going to be my first project," she said.

"Why are you really here?" I asked. "I mean, I'll sell you all the embroidery supplies you need, but if you're here for some other reason, I'd rather have you be up front with me."

"Fair enough. I'm Kendra Morgan, a reporter for the *Tinseltown Tattler*. Like the rest of the journalists in this town, I'm here to find out about the death of Babushka Tru."

"And your investigative skills led you to an embroidery shop five miles away from the scene of the crime?"

"I know your mom is Beverly Singer, the costume designer for Henry Beaumont's new movie, *Sonam Zakaria: A Glamorous Life*," Kendra said. "I also know that she and Babs didn't get along and that they had an argument the morning Babs died."

"I don't know anything about Babs' accident," I said. "I was here when the accident occurred."

"Don't go getting defensive on me. I don't think your mother pushed Babushka Tru out of that loft to her death. In fact, I've tried to tell Detectives Bailey and Ray as much, but they won't listen to me. They think I have some sort of angle."

After hearing that she didn't think my mother was guilty, I offered Kendra a cup of coffee. I didn't entirely trust her, but I wanted to hear what she had to say.

Kendra accepted the coffee, and we sat down in the sit-and-stitch square.

"This is a nice little boutique you have here," she said. "Maybe I could do a piece on it for the *Tattler* . . . you know, if this all turns out well for your mom."

"About that. Why are you so convinced she had nothing to do with Babs' death?"

She leaned forward. "Here's the deal. I've been following a story about Babs and her manager for over a year now. The manager is kind of a father-figure to Babs. But, much like her *real* dad, he'd started taking advantage of her . . . only in more ways than one, if you get my drift."

"I get it," I said.

"Okay, so Babs was starting to get tired of their whole arrangement, and they'd been fighting a lot," Kendra said. "She was getting ready to fire him—I *know* she was. And when that happened, he was going to be ruined."

"Why would he be ruined?"

"Because no one else would've hired him. He's an alcoholic who is also addicted to gambling. Babs had been paying off his poker debts for years. You think anyone else would do that, given the amount of work he does?" She snorted. "Or, should I say, given the amount of work he *doesn't*? Babushka Tru should have been working steadily since *Surf Dad*, but he sat around on his lazy butt and not only didn't get her any substantial work, he got her into alcohol too."

"Why do you think he's the one who killed her?" I asked.

"He was always hanging around her. He was there on set yesterday—I saw him myself." She sat her coffee on the table and spread her hands. "It's like this. He had the most to gain from her death, and the most to lose from her living. It's rumored that Babs was pregnant. If that's the case, I'll bet dollars to donuts that the baby was his. I've already told you that I believe Babs was getting ready to dump the guy. If she did, the money she got for this movie would be his last commission from her. She was poised to make a comeback with this film. She'd have hired a better manager, and he'd have been out."

"You said that Detectives Ray and Bailey won't listen to you," I said. "I'd have thought they'd have to."

"Well, they told me they were looking into everyone who was on the set as a suspect, but they thought I was just there to get some sort of exclusive." She gave me a rueful grin. "People tend not to trust you when you tell them you work for the *Tinseltown Tattler*. Had I said I worked for CNN, I'd have been taken seriously."

"Why are you telling me all this?" I asked.

"Because if my mother was at the top of a list of murder suspects, I'd be making sure the police took a long, hard look at a much likelier suspect."

"Thank you."

She reached into her small, beaded clutch and took out a card. "I'd like for you to call me if you find out anything."

I glanced at the card before putting it in my pocket. "Okay. Thanks again for the input."

"Anytime. I hope you'll return the favor," she said.

"I will if I can."

As Kendra left, she said she might really consider trying embroidery one day and that if she did, she knew where to shop. I still didn't trust her. Like the Tallulah County Police Department detectives, I knew Kendra was simply looking for an exclusive, but the tip about Babs' manager could prove to be valuable information.

I needed to do something to keep my hands busy. I'd finished up my other projects in anticipation of working on the costumes for the movie—all except for the two projects I had ongoing in my two evening classes, and I preferred to work on those then. Now that the movie probably wasn't going to be made, I didn't have the costumes to keep me occupied. I went to the racks and found a beautiful stamped pillowcase kit. Rather than using the threads that came with the kit, however, I decided to do the entire floral design using a soft mauve floss. It would be like redwork or blackwork—a form of embroidery where one uses only black or red thread to create the design—only with mauve. The monochromatic color scheme would match the décor in my bedroom, and it would provide some stitching that I could do without having to think too much . . . about the stitching, anyway.

I found the perfect-colored floss, sat down on a red club chair in the sit-and-stitch square, and began to work. Angus lay down at my feet and chewed on one of his favorite toys—a Kodiak bear that Vera had given him.

I was a little surprised that Vera hadn't been in today. The day was young, though.

The design on the pillowcase consisted mostly of lazy daisy stitches and French knots. I'd done a good-sized portion of the first pillowcase when my next customer came in. Or, at least, she appeared to be a customer. She looked more like a customer than Kendra had. This woman had shoulder-length chestnut hair, brown eyes, and a friendly, open smile.

"Welcome to the Seven-Year Stitch," I said. "How may I help you?"

"I'm looking for some tapestry needles," she said, bending slightly to pet Angus who'd gone over to say hello.

I put my pillowcase on the ottoman and walked over to the counter. "What size?"

"I need a twenty-eight, and a twenty-six, if you have them," she said. "I'm doing some petite cross-stitch on a linen tablecloth for my sister's first wedding anniversary."

I smiled. "I have both sizes." This was more like it.

I was sitting in the sit-and-stitch square dutifully working on my pillowcase—lazy daisy, lazy daisy, French knot, lazy daisy, et cetera—when Alfred breezed into the shop. He looked dapper, carefree, and not like a man recently appointed the task of defending my mother against a murder charge.

"Good afternoon, young man," he said to Angus.

Angus trotted over and dropped a soggy ball at Alfred's polished loafers. Rather than picking it up, Alfred took a dog biscuit wrapped first in a napkin and then in a linen handkerchief and handed it to the dog.

"Your grandma sent you that, Angus." He gave me a wink. "Would she die if she heard me call her that?"

"No," I said, with a laugh. "She loves him to pieces." I placed my pillowcase on the coffee table and offered Alfred a cup of coffee.

"No, thank you, darling. I've already had enough to sink a battleship." He placed his hands on his hips and surveyed the shop. "Excellent! Beautiful place you have here. I'd seen the photos, of course, but they don't do it justice. I'm very proud of you."

"Thank you. Come sit down and tell me why you're so chipper after the super-secret meeting at my kitchen table."

Alfred moved over to the navy sofa facing away from the window and sat down. "I'm in a good mood because your mother isn't guilty, of course."

"You knew that—or, at least, I *hope* you did—when you first arrived this morning, and you didn't seem so carefree then," I said.

He gazed around the room. "I like how you've set this small, cozy area apart from the merchandise. It makes it very welcoming."

"Alfred."

He brought his eyes back to mine. "Everything

your mother said to Cam Whitting and me after you left was told to us in confidence. As her attorneys, we cannot break that confidence."

"I realize that," I said. "But can't you tell me *something* that will ease my mind too? For instance, was my mother in any way responsible for Babushka Tru's death?"

"No, she was not," he said firmly. "However, she believes she might know the identity of the guilty party. That's causing her quite a bit of grief and consternation."

I leaned forward. "But this could clear her as a suspect."

"If anyone else can corroborate her story, then it certainly can," he said, with a smile.

"And you believe someone can?" I asked.

"I do. There were enough people on set that someone had to have seen enough to confirm your mother's . . . alibi . . . I suppose you could say. Cam is checking on that even as we speak." He clapped his hands together. "Now, that's all I can say about that. Show me your office and that notorious storeroom where you found that body the morning after your grand opening soiree."

Ted arrived between twelve thirty and one o'clock that afternoon with sub sandwiches and baked chips. I put the cardboard clock on the door saying

I'd be back in thirty minutes, locked up, and then joined Ted and Angus in my office.

As Ted set out our food, I took two bottles of water from the mini-fridge. "I've had an interesting morning," I told him. "First, a reporter from the *Tinseltown Tattler*—Kendra Morgan—came by. She pretended to be a customer, but she made it obvious in a hurry that she knew nothing about embroidery."

"Did she give you any trouble?" he asked.

I shook my head. "Not really. I didn't appreciate her attempt to deceive me, but she did put a bug in my ear about another possible suspect. She said that Babs had been arguing a lot with her manager lately, and that it was rumored that Babs was getting ready to fire him."

"Keep in mind that she'd already tried to deceive you once. She might've just been feeding you another line so that you'd tell her what you know," Ted said.

"Maybe, but she even mentioned Detectives Bailey and Ray. She said she'd tried to get them to look into the manager as a suspect but that they've refused to speak with her."

He unwrapped his sandwich. "It sounds as if they don't trust her either. I'll talk with them and see what I can find out."

I smiled. "Thank you."

"Don't thank me yet, Inch-High. They're bound

to know you and I are involved, so they might not tell me anything. I imagine they're playing this one fairly close to the vest."

"Still, you can tell them Kendra Morgan was here telling me that she suspects Babs' manager," I said. "Either they'd look at the manager a little closer, or else they'd have you warn me about Kendra. At least, we'd learn *something* from talking with them."

"That's true."

I followed Ted's lead and unwrapped my ham-and-cheese sub. "Kendra had also heard the rumor that Babs was pregnant. She believes that, if the rumor was true, that Babs was carrying her manager's baby."

"Babs was pregnant," Ted said. "The medical examiner confirmed that this morning."

"Can they do a DNA test to determine paternity?" I asked.

"I'm sure they can, but that'll take a while. Still, it adds to motives for murdering Babs that your mother did not have."

"Speaking of Mom, Alfred came in a little while ago. He said that she believes she knows who killed Babs. Apparently, she saw something." I took a drink of my water. "Ted, why is she shutting me out on this? Why won't she tell me anything?"

"I think it's because she's either protecting you

or she's protecting someone else," he said. "Did she ever call Henry back?"

"I don't know." I slowly put the cap back on my water bottle. "Do you think that's it? Do you think Henry killed Babs and that Mom is protecting him?"

Ted placed his strong hand over mine. "Don't get ahead of yourself. Give her a little space, and maybe she'll come around and tell you what she knows."

"And if she doesn't?"

He grinned. "Somehow, you'll find a way to drag it out of her. But go easy on her. Maybe you could just tell her what Kendra Morgan told you, and see what she says about that."

Chapter Twelve

After lunch, I did an Internet search for Babushka Tru's manager. I learned his name was Carl Paxton and that he'd been a corporate attorney before dipping his toe into the entertainment pond. Babs had been his first client. At thirty-five, Paxton was going through a rather messy divorce when he'd renegotiated Babs' contract with the *Surf Dad* producers, garnering the child star a sizable salary increase for what would be the show's final season.

Paxton had a few high-profile celebrity romances, but none of them lasted very long. I could find no other mentions of big-name clients, so I guessed that Babs was the biggest name on his client roster . . . maybe the *only* name.

When Babs turned twenty-one, Carl Paxton took her to the Gallery, a Hollywood club frequented by movie stars and pop music moguls.

Together, they toasted to her adulthood. According to gossip sites—including the *Tinseltown Tattler*—that occasion marked the beginning of Babs' romantic relationship with the manager who was twenty-four years her senior. I, for one, thought it was more than a little creepy. Had this guy been biding his time since the girl was eleven years old to become her boyfriend?

Ignoring the canoodling, *we're-so-in-love* pics and articles, I moved on to the more recent *trouble-in-paradise* exposés. Headlines blared, "Paxton Warns BTru Not to Make Bollywood Film" and wondered, "Is BTru Risking Her Career for Henry Beaumont?" These articles contained photos of a seemingly infatuated Babushka Tru and a besotted, albeit married Henry Beaumont spending more and more time together. Spokespersons for both Babs and Henry contended that they were simply hammering out details and contract negotiations for the upcoming movie role. Still, there were fewer and fewer incidences of Babs and Carl Paxton being seen together, and rumors of a rift were widespread.

Finally, I shut down my computer and returned to the sit-and-stitch square to ruminate on everything while I worked on my pillowcase. Both Angus and Jill agreed with me wholeheartedly that Paxton had been right in trying to dissuade Babs to make her comeback in a biopic that would likely have little commercial appeal. (What? Sometimes it helps you to sort things out by talking them over with pets and/or mannequins. Don't judge.)

Mom hoped the film would appeal to those who determined artistic merit; and while it very well might, small independent productions like this movie can often abound in awards and yet fall flat at the box office. So, from the standpoint of someone managing Babushka Tru's career, I could see why Paxton would have wanted her to find a role that would've had a better chance at becoming a blockbuster—like a romantic comedy or an action flick. Had Babs' affection for Henry Beaumont colored her decision making? Had Henry promised her great things? Had Babs fallen so far from grace in the eyes of Hollywood that she'd had practically no choice but to take this role in order to prove herself?

I was deciding that if anyone could answer those questions for me, Mom could, when a customer walked through the door. She was a woman in her mid- to late thirties, and she was searching for a book with projects combining cross-stitch with beading.

I took her over to the issues of Jill Oxton's *Cross Stitch & Beading* magazines I had on hand. "I also have some kits that combine cross-stitching and beading."

"That would be great," she said.

I led her to the kits. "If you need any help, just let me know."

"I think I'll get one of these kits to get the hang of things, but I want one of the magazines too. I'm enamored of the tiger in that one." She pointed to the cover of one of the issues of *Cross Stitch & Beading*.

"Do you need any floss or needles while you're here?" I asked.

"Not yet. Everything I'll need for this one is included, isn't it?" She held up the kit she'd chosen of an angel.

"Yes. The kit is complete."

"Then I'll start with that and then come back for supplies for other projects if I do all right with this one," she said, with a laugh.

We walked over to the counter.

"If you need any help at all, please come back and I'll give you a hand," I said.

"I will. Thank you."

I checked out her purchases and placed them in a periwinkle Seven-Year Stitch bag. "Thank *you*. I hope to see you again soon."

As she was walking out, Mita Trublonski walked in. She was wearing the halfhearted "disguise" of mirrored sunglasses. In fact, I only realized the glasses were supposed to be a disguise when she took them off and apologized for the crazy getup. The rest of the disguise consisted of a pastel polka dot umbrella—after all, it *was* cloudy and looked like it might rain—a pair of black leather pants, and a boxy, white Chanel jacket.

Had anyone *not* seen through Ms. Trublonski's disguise, the pack of reporters who'd trailed her to the Seven-Year Stitch would've been a dead giveaway. Fortunately, the reporters stayed outside on the street. Unfortunately, they and their flashing cameras caused Angus to go on a barking, jumping-at-the-window rampage and prevented patrons from getting anywhere near my shop.

"I'm calling the police!" I yelled, taking my phone from my jeans pocket and showing the group standing at the window that I had punched the numbers nine-one-one into the phone. "If you don't disperse from in front of this shop in the next ten seconds, I *will* call the police and I *will* press charges!"

I really would have called the police, but I was bluffing about pressing charges. I had no idea what charges I could possibly press, but my threat worked. The reporters moved away from the shop. Some moved along the street on either side—toward MacKenzies' Mochas to the left and the aromatherapy shop to the right—while the rest went across the street to watch the Seven-Year Stitch from in front of the Brew Crew.

"I'm glad you didn't have to call in the cavalry," Ms. Trublonski said, as Angus eventually calmed. "I feel I've brought too much attention and aggravation to you and your mother already."

"No, that's fine," I said. "I'm sorry you're being followed and hounded while you're still trying to come to terms with your grief."

"Yes, well. . . ." She stole a glance at the media stationed outside Todd's pub and craft brewery. "It goes with the territory . . . even when you're not the famous one." She gestured toward the sit-and-stitch square. "May we sit?"

"Let's go into my office where we can better avoid the prying eyes," I said.

"Sure," she said, and yet she looked over her shoulder at the reporters again.

I led her into my office. "Would you care for some water, mango juice, or soda?"

"No, thanks. I won't stay but a minute. I just wanted to say I'm sorry for all the sorrow this tragedy has brought on your mom . . . and you too, of course."

"We're sorry for *your* grief, Ms. Trublonski."

"Thank you. You're kind." She raised an index finger. "I'll have to mention that in the book."

"The book?" I asked.

"Yes. Carl—Carl Paxton, Babs' manager—came by with breakfast this morning, and we had an in-depth discussion about my writing a book. And

we're going to do it," she said. "We're going to pro-
duce a book—I'll be doing most of the writing—
and we're going to call it *BTru to Your Dreams*. Get
it? *BTru*—like the media dubbed Babs?"

I nodded. "I get it."

"Carl said it would be an excellent way to deal
with my sorrow while also making sure Babs'
story is properly told."

I struggled for the proper words. "Are you sure
you want to write a book? I mean, maybe you
should give yourself time to get over the shock of
your daughter's death before you rush into anything."

"Oh, no, it's a done deal. Carl is probably
shopping the literary and film rights even as we
speak. He said we need to get the jump on those
media hounds who'll be eager to write their own
books and tell their own twisted version of Babs'
story." She gave one resolute nod. "I'm going to
do this for her. I owe her that."

After Mita Trublonski left, I returned to the sit-
and-stitch square and embroidered the pillowcase. I made good progress on it. I also waited on
a few customers and took a couple of phone
calls. One caller wanted to make sure class was
still on for this evening, and I verified that it was.
Upon ending the call, I reflected that it might

have been a reporter rather than a student. I hoped that wasn't the case, but I'd deal with class after work.

Just when I thought I couldn't possibly be surprised by anything else life threw at me that day, Henry Beaumont called.

"Hi . . . Henry," I stammered after he introduced himself. "How may I help you?"

"I'd like for you to meet with me," he said. "I'm in my car now and can be there within a couple of minutes."

"Okay, but come to the back of the shop. There's an alley there, and I'll let you in the back entrance. Maybe that way, you won't be mobbed by reporters."

"Is the media staking out your place?" he asked.

"They're not as obtrusive now as they were earlier," I said. "But I don't doubt they're still around here somewhere."

"All right. Thanks. I'll be right there."

"I'll be watching for you."

I put aside my embroidery and went to the back entrance of the shop. Almost immediately, a silver Mercedes sedan pulled into the alley. The windows were slightly tinted, but when the car got closer, I could see that Henry was driving it.

He parked, got out, and looked around. I assumed he was checking for media.

"I appreciate your meeting with me, Marcy," he said, as he walked through the door.

"Anytime." I locked the door back after we were inside. "So, what can I do for you?"

He sighed. "I'd appreciate it if you'd try to talk your mother into speaking with me. I've left message after message, but she won't return my calls."

I remembered what Alfred said about Mom knowing something about Babs' murder. Could she have seen Henry with Babs after the fitting?

"I'll talk with her," I said. I led him through the hall and into my office. "Would you like something to drink?"

"No, I'm fine. Thank you, though." He sank into the chair in front of my desk. He looked gaunt and exhausted, and his eyes bore no hint of exotic color from tinted contact lenses.

"You haven't been sleeping, have you?" I asked.

"Not very much."

"What happened that morning? Did you see either Mom or Babs after you sent Mom to do the refitting?"

"I saw your mother." He raised his eyes to mine. "What has she told you about that morning?"

"Not much," I said. "In fact, this is typical Mom. When she's in crisis mode, she practically shuts down and doesn't talk much to anyone." That sounded like a reasonable version of the truth that could explain why she hadn't returned Henry's calls. "All I know is that Mom did the refitting and that she and Babs argued about it."

Henry rubbed his hand over his face. "I don't think she meant to do it, but I believe that altercation led to Babs' fall."

"You believe my mother had something to do with Babs' death?" Was he simply trying to point the finger at Mom in order to exonerate himself?

"Not purposely, no," he said. "I just think that they got into an argument, that there was some pushing involved, and that Babs lost her footing and fell."

I stared at him openmouthed.

Henry stood and placed his hands on my shoulders. "I need to talk with her. I must know what happened if I'm going to be of any help whatsoever."

He pulled me into a hug, but my arms hung limply at my sides. I was still processing what he was saying.

"I'm doing a press conference at five thirty this afternoon outside the hotel where I'm staying," he said, stepping back to look into my face. "I'm unable to wait any longer. The press is calling for answers."

"A-and you're going to tell them your theory . . . about Mom?"

"No, no, no. I'm going to answer any questions about Babs' death as elusively as I possibly can," Henry said. "But I need to know for my own personal reasons what happened."

"Because of your relationship with Babs?" I asked.

"Because of my relationship with your mother. The show must go on, you know."

"The show must go on?" I echoed. "But how can it?"

"I'm too heavily invested in this project not to get another actress and move on, Marcy, and I need to be assured I can count on Bev as my costume designer. If I can't, I'm going to have to find a replacement for her too, and as soon as possible." He looked at his watch. "I need to go and get ready for the press conference. Have her call me, okay?"

I nodded. "I'll do my best."

"Tell her that if I don't hear from her by noon tomorrow, I'll have to hire another costumer." That said, he left.

After Henry left the office, I sat down on my desk chair and placed my head between my knees. I felt light-headed and was afraid I might faint. Could this nightmare get any weirder?

The bells over the shop door jingled, and I groaned.

"Be there in a minute!" I shouted.

"How about I come to you?" The deep, rich

voice belonged to Todd Calloway. I was so relieved, I thought I might cry.

"Thank goodness, it's you," I said.

"What's wrong?" He sidestepped Angus, who'd trotted in beside him, and dropped to one knee in front of me. "Are you sick?"

"I don't know if sick is the proper word for what I'm feeling," I said. "Although, come to think of it, I do feel like I'm against the ropes and being beaten by a professional boxer . . . just one blow after another."

"Wanna talk about it?" he asked.

"I'm sure you've heard most of it. Babushka Tru died on set. Mom was overheard arguing with her before her death. Her mother visited both yesterday and today and is getting ready to write a tell-all book. And now the producer-director—Henry Beaumont—just left after telling me that he believes Mom is responsible for Babs' death but that he needs to know by noon tomorrow whether or not he needs to hire a new costume designer. And if that's not enough, Mom is shutting me out and won't tell me what's going on with her."

"Wow. You don't need me. You need a bottle of vodka."

I laughed. "No, I don't. I couldn't handle a hangover on top of all my other problems."

"I made you smile, though." He grinned. "You got to give me credit for that."

"Yes, you did," I said. "Thank you. Now, what are you doing here? Are you looking for a new embroidery project already?"

"Nope, I believe I've got all the embroidery supplies I'll need . . . ever," Todd said. "I just came to check on you after seeing all the vultures swarming outside the pub earlier today."

"I'm sorry about that. They were standing outside the window driving Angus and me up the wall until I threatened to call the police. If they bother you again, threaten them. That seems to work."

He shook his head. "I won't threaten. I'll simply tell them to either buy a drink or leave."

"I know some of the reporters have been asking Blake and Sadie questions," I said. "Have they been pestering you?"

"Nah. I hear them talking among themselves, but they haven't talked to me much."

I studied his face. "Are you downplaying it to make me feel better?"

"Of course I am." He took my hands and pulled me to my feet. "But I can handle whatever they throw at me, and so can you. Stop your moping."

"You're right."

"I always am. We'll get through this. We've gotten through worse, haven't we?" he asked.

"Yeah. We've gotten through worse."

Chapter Thirteen

When Angus and I arrived home after work that evening, we found Mom sitting on the sofa in the living room. She wasn't watching television, wasn't reading, wasn't thumbing through a magazine—she was just sitting there staring into space.

"Hello, darling," she said, as I followed Angus into the living room. He'd already placed his big, furry head on her lap, and she was hugging him.

"What's up?" I asked.

"Nothing. Did you have a nice day?"

I sat on the armchair, slipped off my shoes, and propped my feet on the ottoman. "I'm not sure I'd call it *nice*. It has been one surprise after another, though."

"I should get dinner started," she said.

"No need, unless you're hungry," I said. "I'll

just grab a protein bar on the way back to the shop."

"Ted isn't joining us?"

"No. He has to work this evening." I glanced at the clock over the mantel and saw that it was twenty minutes past five. Henry's press conference was due to start in ten minutes. "Mom, why won't you return Henry's calls?"

"I've been distracted. Besides, Ted said I shouldn't speak with another suspect, right?"

"He did say that, but what advice did Alfred and Cam give you? If you're still going to work with the man, you'll have to speak with him sooner or later. That doesn't mean you have to discuss Babushka Tru's death."

"Why the sudden concern over Henry?" she asked.

"He came by the shop today and practically begged me to have you call him." When she didn't respond, I felt I had to bring out the big guns in order to see how she was really feeling. "He thinks you might've accidentally caused Babs to fall."

Mom's jaw dropped. "He's pointing the finger at *me*? He was the last person to see Babs alive. I'll bet he didn't tell you *that* now, did he?"

"No, he didn't. So you think Henry killed Babs?"

"I'm not saying that," she said, sighing and resting her head against the back of the sofa. "I don't know what I think. All I know is that I was on my way back to report to Henry when I passed him heading toward the loft's fitting room."

"Are you sure he was going to see Babs?"

"I'm not certain, but where else could he have been going? The fitting area was the only thing in that direction."

"Maybe the two of you should talk," I said. "You could have Alfred with you, if you think it's necessary. I mean, isn't it possible that both of you are mistaken and that neither of you caused Babs to fall? Maybe there's something else that, if you put your heads together, you'll remember." Again, I glanced at the clock.

"Why do you keep watching the clock? I didn't think you had to be back at the shop until six o'clock."

"I don't, but Henry is giving a press conference outside his hotel at five thirty." I retrieved the television remote. "I think we should watch and see what he has to say."

Mom was silent, but she didn't protest. She merely sat with her arms crossed over her chest. Angus came over to lie by my chair.

I turned on the television and switched back and forth between the three local channels until I found the one that was stationed outside Henry Beaumont's hotel. The stiff-haired anchorwoman was already talking.

". . . where Henry Beaumont, the award-winning Hollywood producer and director of such movies as *Fatal Lies*, will be discussing the tragic death of starlet Babushka Tru, who died while on location for Beaumont's latest movie, *Sonam Zakaria: A Glamorous Life*. Here comes Mr. Beaumont now. Let's listen."

The camera panned to a podium with a microphone that had been set up on the lawn of the hotel. Reporters were gathered four deep in a semicircle around the podium.

Henry had changed clothes since he'd been at the Seven-Year Stitch. He was dressed in a tailored suit, and I wouldn't have been surprised to learn that he'd had one of the makeup artists touch up his haggard complexion. His eyes appeared to be an emerald green, which meant he was back in contact lens mode.

He stepped up to the podium and adjusted both his tie and the microphone. "Good evening. Thank you all for being here. First and foremost, I want to express my deepest sympathies—as well as those of the entire cast and crew—to Babushka Tru's family and friends. She was a beautiful person, and she'll be terribly missed. Since her death is still under investigation by the Tallulah County Police Department, however, I'm not permitted to speak about that and will take no questions on the subject."

From the corner of my eye, I sneaked a peek at Mom. She was glaring at the TV screen, and her mouth was a thin, tight line.

"Further, I must say that although we are all appalled and shocked by Babushka Tru's untimely death, the production will go forward as planned. As soon as the investigation into this affair has been completed to the point that we may return to San Francisco, the cast and crew will go back and regroup, recast the role of Sonam Zakaria, and continue making the film. We know Babs would have wanted it that way, and we'll, of course, dedicate the movie to her memory." He lowered his head briefly. Then he said, "That's all I have to say for now. Thank you for your time." With that, he turned and hurried back into the hotel.

The camera went back to the anchorwoman. "There you have it. The show must go on, I suppose. Doug?"

The screen split into the shot of the anchorwoman at the scene and "Doug" who was sitting at the news desk.

"Lynette, what did you make of Henry Beaumont's demeanor?"

"I think the man looked exhausted, Doug. He has obviously been through an ordeal. He lost his star, but it sounds as if he has too much invested in this movie to back out."

"I understand that Mita Trublonski, Babushka

Tru's mother, is in town," Doug said. "Any word from her on how she feels about Beaumont's decision to continue making the movie?"

"Not yet. I do plan on following up with her and will be sure and keep our viewers informed," Lynette said.

"Lynette, what do you make of the fact that Ms. Trublonski has been to a local embroidery shop—the Seven-Year Stitch—twice since coming to Tallulah Falls?" Doug asked.

"One could surmise that the woman enjoys embroidery, Doug, but I'm not so sure that's the case. The shop owner is Marcella Singer, daughter of the movie's costume designer, Beverly Singer."

Before Lynette could continue, I switched the television off.

"What did they mean that Mita Trublonski has been to your shop twice?" Mom asked. "I thought yesterday was the first time she'd been there."

"It was. She came back today. I've got to say those people are quick."

"What did she want?"

"She said she came to apologize for any grief last night's visit might've caused," I said. "But she also mentioned that she and Carl Paxton are writing a book about Babs' life. Mom, have you met this Paxton character?"

Mom nodded. "I don't particularly like him, though. He hasn't done anything to make me dislike him, it's just that I get a bad vibe when I'm around him."

"First thing this morning, Kendra Morgan—a reporter with the *Tinseltown Tattler*—came into the Seven-Year Stitch. At first, she tried to play herself off as a customer, but when she couldn't pull it off, she came clean and told me why she was really there."

"I've met Kendra," Mom said. "She hangs around movie sets all the time. She isn't a bad sort, considering the work she does. She could be a decent reporter if she'd apply herself."

"Well, Kendra seems to think that Carl might've killed Babs. She says they'd been having arguments and that she'd heard that Babs was going to fire Carl after this movie," I said. "She also seemed to think Carl might be the father of Babs' baby."

"So it's been confirmed that Babs *was* pregnant?" she asked.

"Yeah. Ted told me this morning."

She frowned. "I'm sorry about that. I really had thought she was just enjoying the buffet a little too much."

"But what about Carl?" I asked. "Do you think he might've been capable of knocking Babs in the head and then pushing her off that ledge? Was he hanging around the set that morning?"

"Yes, he was there." She shrugged. "I guess anything's possible."

"You still think it was Henry, don't you?"

"I don't know what to think," she said softly.

I sighed. "You need to talk with him, Mom. Or, at least, have Alfred let him know whether or not you're still interested in designing the costumes for the movie. He told me that if he hasn't heard from you by noon tomorrow, he'll have to hire another costumer."

"Okay. Thanks for passing that information along."

"What are you going to do?" I asked.

She shrugged, stood, and went upstairs. She was withdrawing again. Part of me wanted to go after her and tell her that she couldn't retreat from this situation, that she had to meet it head-on. But I let her go.

I sighed again, kissed Angus on the head, and then went into the kitchen to fill his bowl with kibble.

As I unlocked the door to the Seven-Year Stitch, I heard Sadie call my name.

"Hey," she said breathlessly. "I'm glad I could catch you before the students got here. How are you and your mom holding up?"

"Not so hot." I held the door open for Sadie, and she stepped through and flipped on the lights.

"Anything I can do?" she asked.

"Not unless you're psychic. Mom seems to think Henry Beaumont might've pushed Babs to her death. Henry thinks Mom *accidentally contributed* to Babs' fall. And a tabloid reporter is absolutely certain Babs' manager, Carl Paxton, is the murderer." I flopped the tote bag containing my crewel project onto the counter. "I tried to encourage Mom to talk with Henry—with Alfred present, if she preferred—so the two of them could put their heads together and see what one might've noticed that the other missed, and vice versa."

"That makes sense," Sadie said. "Maybe together they could come up with something important that they'd both thought was inconsequential before."

"See? I knew you'd understand." I turned my palms up. "She won't do it, though. And she might lose her spot as costume designer on this movie."

"I'd hate for her to do that if it turns out Henry is innocent."

"So would I," I said. "She had such high hopes for the movie. She's won some minor awards before, but this movie had some serious big-award buzz. It could be huge for her. On the other hand, Henry might be a killer."

"There is that. But I get the feeling you think Henry is innocent."

"I do, Sadie. I don't know why, but I don't think he's our guy. I need to talk with Carl Paxton and see what kind of feeling I get from him."

"I'm not so sure that's a good idea," Sadie said. "What possible excuse could you come up with for talking with him?"

I thought about it a second, and then I grinned. "He talked Mita Trublonski into doing a book about Babs' life. I'll ask him about doing a book about Mom."

"Knowing you, you might be able to pull it off. Oops, I see some of your students headed this way. I'll talk with you later." She gave me a quick hug. "Just be careful. Okay?"

"Always."

The crewel class went well, despite the fact that a small portion of my brain was still trying to unravel the tangled skein of yarn that led to Babushka Tru's killer. As soon as my last student was out the door, I took Deputy Preston's card from my desk drawer and called him.

"Robert Preston," he answered.

"Hi, Deputy Preston. It's Marcy Singer."

"Oh, hey, Marcy! How are you? I hope the media isn't giving you fits."

"Not too bad," I said. "I did have one slip in under the radar this morning. She pretended to be an embroidery enthusiast, but I could tell right away that she wasn't."

"And then you sent her packing?" he asked.

"Not right away. She had something interesting to tell me." I went on to explain how Kendra thought Carl Paxton might've been involved in Babs' death. "She said she'd taken her theories to Detectives Bailey and Ray, but they blew her off. They think she's either making it up or trying to get some sort of exclusive."

"It's not like Bailey or Ray to ignore a lead," Deputy Preston said. "I'm sure they followed up on it but didn't feel inclined to share their information with Ms. Morgan."

"You're probably right. Did you happen to see Carl Paxton on the movie set that morning?"

"I'm not that familiar with many of the movie people—only the major players," he said. "I'll look him up on the Internet, though, and I'll ask the other guys who were on guard Monday if they happened to see anything."

"Thank you so much," I said. "I truly appreciate your help."

"Hey, that's what I'm here for. Thanks for the tip. Um, do me a favor, though. If I find anything out, please don't share it with any reporters."

"I sure won't."

As I ended the call, I saw Ted nearing the shop.

I opened the door and greeted him with a hug and kiss.

"Thanks," he said. "I needed that."

"I needed it more."

He was immediately on high alert. "Did something happen?" He looked around the shop.

"Everything is fine," I said. "It's just been a long hard day." I gave him the CliffsNotes version of my day.

"Why don't you lock up, and let's go for a walk on the beach?" Ted asked.

"I really need to get home to Mom. . . ."

"She'll be fine for a few minutes. We won't stay long." He took my hand. "We can take off our shoes and wade in the surf. It'll do us both good."

I smiled. "You always know just what to say."

I locked up the Seven-Year Stitch, leaving Jill in charge until morning, and handed Ted the keys to my Jeep.

"You drive," I said. "I want to relax and be chauffeured."

He drove us to a small public beach where a group of college students had built a campfire. They were roasting marshmallows and invited us to join them for a beer as we passed.

"Maybe later," Ted said.

He'd left his jacket and tie in the Jeep, and he'd

undone the first four buttons of his now untucked shirt.

"It feels kinda strange to be at the beach without Angus," I said.

"I believe he'd forgive us just this once . . . but don't tell him."

"I won't unless he asks." I smiled and slipped off my shoes.

Ted took off his shoes and socks and put the socks inside the shoes. We rolled our pants up to our calves, and then walked hand in hand to the water's edge. The huge crags loomed out of the water like some sort of benevolent sea monsters as the foam lapped at our ankles. I looked over at Ted and laughed, and for an instant, the moon peeped out from behind a cloud.

For a moment, I could forget about Babushka Tru, and Carl Paxton, and Mita Trublonski, and Henry Beaumont. For that brief interlude, I was just a girl falling in love. Too bad the moment couldn't last.

Chapter Fourteen

That night when Ted and I got to my house, Vera's silver BMW was parked in the driveway. I'd found it odd that she hadn't stopped by the shop today, especially given her interest in Babushka Tru and the girl's mysterious death. I thought she'd come by today if for no other reason than to learn what Mita Trublonski had said to Mom.

I parked the Jeep, and Ted pulled in behind me.

"I hope Vera isn't badgering Mom to tell her about her visit with Ms. Trublonski," I said to Ted when he got out of his car.

"I imagine Vera would be a little more subtle than that," he said. "Although, you never know."

When we went inside, I was shocked and angry to find that Vera had brought along her boyfriend, reporter Paul Samms. Upon hearing my sharp intake of breath, Ted squeezed my hand.

"Get a handle on the situation before you react," he said under his breath.

I nodded.

"Hey, guys," Ted said with a smile. "Vera, I didn't know you and Paul were waiting here on Marcy, or I wouldn't have kept her out past class time."

"Oh, we haven't been here long," Vera said. "I just wanted to check on Marcy and Beverly. Paul allowed me to canvass the crime scene with him this morning—it was so exciting—and then I bought a notebook and jotted down my observations."

"Uh-oh. Do I need to be concerned about my job security?" Ted asked.

"You don't," said Paul. "But I might. She has the makings of an excellent reporter . . . or novelist."

Paul was a nice-looking older man who would look even better if he weren't so concerned about his age. Rather than letting his hair go John Forsythe gray, he kept it dyed a dark brown. And the skin was so taut around his eyes, that I was sure he'd had some type of surgery—either nip and tuck or a dermal filler. Not that there was anything wrong with the man trying to look his best—he kept in excellent shape and dressed as if Tim Gunn were in charge of his wardrobe—but somehow it seemed strange for the man to be that concerned about aging. We, as a society, expect women to try to stay forever young. But men are allowed to age. They become "more rugged" or "interesting." Women become "wrinkled" or they "let themselves go." Great, now I felt guilty for passing judgment on Paul for trying to look his best.

"What crime scene were you investigating?" I asked.

"Ford's Mill," Paul said. "The movie set . . . the area surrounding where the body was found. . . ."

As if I didn't know.

"Now that the movie has stopped production, at least temporarily, there weren't that many officers around," he continued. "And the ones that were there didn't have a problem with us poking around as long as we stayed away from the areas that were cordoned off. I primarily wanted to investigate the area around where the body of the gunman who shot at you was found, Ted."

Now I had guilt for rushing to judgment about Paul on two counts.

"Manu and I were all over that area on Monday," Ted said. "We didn't find much of any consequence."

"I'd have thought you'd be investigating Babs' death," I said.

"Well, I *am* interested in Babs' death," Paul said. "But while that's important, I feel that the people of Tallulah Falls and Tallulah County will be more impacted by what we learn about this gunman.

We need to find his partner, or else that threat is still out there."

"I agree wholeheartedly," Ted said, sitting on the sofa beside Paul. "Did you find anything?"

"I did," Vera said, getting out of her chair to come over and present her prize to Ted. "It's some sort of medallion or button or something."

I was sitting on the arm of the sofa beside Ted, so I looked over his shoulder to examine the small, round brass disk. There was no design on it whatsoever other than the letters TCMSA.

"What does TCMSA stand for?" I asked.

"I'd imagine the A is for an association of some sort," Mom said. I wondered if Vera had noticed how uncharacteristically quiet she was being.

"I'll check into it when I get to work tomorrow," Ted said.

"Are you going to admit it into evidence?" Vera asked. "Have it dusted for prints, maybe? I picked it up with a tissue, so my prints aren't on it."

And yet she'd handed the button to Ted, and he was now examining it; so both their prints were on it now.

"I'm sure the crime scene techs will give it a thorough exam." Ted hid a grin. "What else did you notice, Paul? Um . . . and you too, Vera?"

"Well, it was a good time to look around because the place is all but deserted now," Paul said. "Most of the reporters are staking out Henry

Beaumont, Mita Trublonski, and other cast and crew members who are staying in town."

"Yes, there were only a couple deputies there when we were on the scene," Vera said.

Paul smiled at her. "I can hardly wait to read the rest of your report."

Vera actually blushed.

"If you'll all excuse me, I think I'll let Angus inside and then go on up to bed," Mom said.

"Good night," Vera said.

"We should go," Paul said.

"Yes, I suppose we should." Vera stood. "Ted, you'll let me know what you find out about the button, won't you?"

"Of course," he said.

"Thank you for coming to check on Mom," I said to Vera.

"She's not herself at all," Vera said. "I realize she's been through a terrible ordeal, but maybe you should have her talk with someone. If you need the name of a good therapist, I know one who's located in Lincoln City."

"Thanks."

By the time Angus came bounding into the living room, Vera and Paul had left. Mom trailed listlessly behind the dog.

I gave Angus a hug and then let him go over to greet Ted.

"Mom, are you all right?" I asked.

"I'm just tired. I wasn't expecting company this evening."

"I wasn't either, or else Ted and I wouldn't have stopped by the beach on the way home."

"I've set up a meeting with Henry," she said. "Alfred and I are having breakfast with him tomorrow."

"That's good," I said. "If the two of you put your heads together, maybe you can determine who killed Babs."

"Yeah. Let's hope." She didn't sound convincing.

"Are you *that* certain Henry killed her?" I asked. "Because if you are, you don't need to be meeting with him. You need to quit the picture, talk with the police about your suspicions, and move on."

"The only thing I'm certain of right now, Marcella, is that I'm tired, and I need to go to bed." She left the living room and headed for the stairs as I stood speechless watching her go.

I turned to Ted. "Did you hear that? Can you believe her?"

"Stress does different things to different people," he said. "Give her a day or two, and she'll be fine."

"If you say so."

As soon as I got to the shop Thursday morning, I called Mita Trublonski at her hotel.

"Good morning," I said when Ms. Trublonski came on the line. "It's Marcy Singer. I hope I'm not disturbing you."

"No, of course not." Her voice was guarded, as if I might, in fact actually be disturbing her.

"I won't keep you but a second. I was hoping you'd give me Carl Paxton's phone number."

"You want to speak with Carl?" she asked. "Whatever for?"

"After listening to you talk about the book you're writing about your daughter, I thought it might be fun to write something about Mom . . . you know, some of her anecdotes . . . a tribute, in a way, though nothing compared to what you're doing for Babs."

Mita Trublonski was quiet for so long, I was afraid we'd been disconnected.

"Hello?" I asked.

"Yes, dear, I'm here. It's just . . . well, I'm simply surprised by your sudden ambition, that's all. Do you really think a book about a costume designer would sell?"

"That's what I plan to ask Mr. Paxton," I said. "I mean, it wouldn't be *entirely* about Mom. The anecdotes would include her experiences with some of Hollywood's most elite."

"Right."

"Again, it won't be near the blockbuster your book will be." I found myself trying to reassure her once again. She seemed either dubious or threatened by my book idea. Maybe I should've told her I hoped to break into show business and that I was hoping Paxton would represent me. "Mr. Paxton will likely tell me I'm wasting my time, but I'd just like to hear it from a professional, you know?"

"Of course. Hold on."

I paced in front of the counter while I waited for Ms. Trublonski to return to the phone and supply me with the cell phone number of Carl Paxton. After she gave it to me, I read it back to her to make sure I had it right.

"That's it," she said. "Tell him I sent you his way. Maybe he'll be kinder then. He can be a bit like a bulldog in a silk scarf, but he's a good ally if he believes in you."

"Thank you," I said. As I ended the call, I was still puzzling over her comparison—a bulldog in a silk scarf? I supposed it was Ms. Trublonski's way of saying Paxton was rough around the edges.

I called Mr. Paxton's number. The call went to voice mail. I introduced myself and left my cell phone number. I indicated I'd like to buy him lunch and talk over a proposed project that I'd discussed with Mita Trublonski.

I figured that either he would call Ms. Trublonski or she would call him prior to our talking anyway, so my tipping him off to having discussed the book with Ms. Trublonski would speed up that aspect of the game. Whether Ms. Trublonski thought a book about my mother would sell or not, I knew that Paxton would be looking for new clients. Even if the rumor was untrue that Babs had been going to fire the manager after completing her current project, her death had left him without his most profitable client. Sentiment aside, he had to have been looking for more revenue streams.

A customer came in seeking an embroidery starter kit for her young niece. I had some inexpensive needlepoint kits that contained blunted, plastic needles, plastic canvas, and enough yarn to complete the project. I led the elegant woman to the kits.

"These will be wonderful for her," she said, as she paid for her purchase. She patted Angus's head and set his tail to wagging even harder than it already had been before she breezed out the door.

I stepped into my office and called Sadie before another customer came by.

"Hi," I said. "If I come over there for lunch with a strange guy, would you please seat me at the most private table possible?"

"Yeeeah. What are you up to?"

I explained that Carl Paxton was Babs' manager

and that Kendra Morgan believed him to have been involved in her death.

"Hon, you know she's a tabloid reporter," Sadie said. "She was probably just trying to get you to say something she could quote you on."

"Maybe so, but I'm going to try to talk with him anyway. I'm pretending I want to write a book about Mom's experiences in Hollywood."

"And what does Ted think about being stood up in favor of a murder suspect?" she asked.

"One, he doesn't know I might be having lunch with Carl . . . at least, not yet. And two, he and Manu have returned to the crime scene to snoop around a little more, so he couldn't have lunch with me today anyway."

"But I didn't think the Babushka Tru death was their case."

"It isn't," I said. "They're looking at the first crime scene—the one Reggie and I stumbled over before the movie crew got there. Paul Samms and Vera went out there yesterday."

"Did they find anything?"

"A disk that had the initials TCMSA on it. Does that mean anything to you?" I asked.

"No. Should it?"

"I doubt it. It's like Ted said, anyone could've lost a button out there. It could've been a hiker who lost the button a year ago, or it could've fallen off the gunman himself," I said. "Still, now that the Tallulah County Police Department has pulled out all but a couple of cursory guards at the place, Ted and Manu want to see what they can find."

"Yeah, I imagine the Tallulah County boys didn't appreciate our Tallulah Falls guys stepping on their toes on that one, even if it was our guys' case to begin with."

"You're probably right." I got a beep. "I'm getting another call. If I come in, will you put me at the most private table you've got?"

"Yeah . . . private . . . but where Blake and I can keep an eye on you."

"Thanks." I switched from Sadie's call to the incoming call. "This is Marcy Singer. Thank you for calling the Seven-Year Stitch. How may I help you?"

"Hi there, Ms. Singer. This is Carl Paxton returning your call."

"I appreciate your getting back to me so promptly," I said. "Yesterday Mita Trublonski was in my shop, and she was telling me about the book she's writing about her daughter's life. I got to thinking that my mom's experiences designing costumes for some of Hollywood's A-listers might make a good memoir. What do you think?"

"And your mother is Beverly Singer?" he asked.

"That's right."

"Tell me one of these anecdotes."

He was testing me. My mind raced to come up

with something good . . . something involving a popular actor that would be tame enough not to get us sued should we actually write a book and yet juicy enough to be interesting.

"There are so many," I said. "Like the time Brandi Chastain had a conniption because every single scene containing the wine-colored tea-length gown she adored and looked so magnificent wearing had been cut from the movie. She didn't know until she saw the movie's premiere in London—it was the first time she'd seen the finished product—and after dressing down the director, she left the theater in tears."

"Hmm. Interesting. What else have you got?"

"Um, there was the time Jimmy Gless's girdle burst at the seams and his beer gut jutted out from under his shirt," I said.

Paxton laughed. "Oh my goodness, that's great! He always looks trim in his movies. I mean, barrel-chested but not fat."

"Now you know why."

"What time can we meet for lunch?" he asked.

We made arrangements to meet at twelve thirty at MacKenzies' Mochas.

Chapter Fifteen

I got to MacKenzies' Mochas about ten minutes early to make sure Sadie had secured Carl Paxton and me a table with a modicum of privacy. She had.

"Thank you so much," I told her. "When he gets here, point him in my direction."

"What does he look like?" she asked.

I frowned slightly. "I'm not entirely sure. The pictures I saw of him online were mainly of him cuddling Babushka Tru, so there wasn't a straight-on shot. But I think he has blond hair . . . unless he's changed it."

"Marcy!"

"Well, hopefully, he'll ask for me," I said. "And if he doesn't, and you see someone looking as if they're waiting on somebody, point him in my direction."

Sadie shook her head and went to get me a diet soda.

It was good I'd arrived ten minutes early, because Carl Paxton arrived five minutes later. He strode up to the bar in a camel sport jacket and told Blake he was looking for Marcy Singer. Blake pointed him in the right direction.

Carl was an attractive man . . . in a way. I mean, he had the attributes of a hot guy—athletic build, nice hair (yes, it was still blond), brown eyes, broad smile—but there was something about his demeanor that made me cringe. It was almost as if he had a pair of those novelty X-ray glasses that promised boys they could use them to see girls' underwear . . . except it felt to me like Carl Paxton might be wearing invisible X-ray glasses that could see into your soul. I nearly squirmed in my seat.

He held out his hand, and I hesitated slightly.

"I'm Carl Paxton," he said.

"Of course." I finally took his outstretched hand. "And I'm Marcy Singer."

"Yes, the gentleman at the bar pointed you out to me." He turned and gave Blake a little wave.

Blake was looking at me to make sure everything was all right, so I gave him a smile and a nod.

As soon as Carl was seated, Sadie came over and took his drink order.

"So tell me more about this book you're writing," he said, once Sadie had gone to get his ice water.

"Well, I haven't started writing it yet," I said. "I actually hadn't even considered it until Mita Trublonski was in my shop yesterday telling me about the book *she's* writing. Do you think it would sell well?"

"Mita's book?" he asked. "Oh, definitely . . . everyone is curious about Babs right now."

"Um . . . I meant *my* book . . . the book about my mom."

"Oh!" He chuckled. "I don't know yet. That's why I need to hear more about it."

Sadie returned with Carl's water and took our food orders. I got my usual—homemade chicken salad croissant, because they're out-of-this-world good—and Carl got a Caesar salad.

Since I hadn't fully fleshed out my so-called book idea and wasn't really interested in doing so, I turned the conversation back to Mita Trublonski and Babs. "Don't you find it odd that Ms. Trublonski is already considering a book when Babs hasn't even been buried yet?"

Carl's smile faded and his eyes hardened. "She needs to beat every other jerk out there to the punch. There are ruthless people out there who'd publish a pack of lies about Babs, and because they had no other alternative, Babs' fans would gobble it up. Mita is giving the people the truth—a grieving mother's truth. Which would you rather read?"

"Naturally, I'd rather read her mother's account of her life," I said, thinking that I wouldn't spend my money on a book about Babushka Tru because the only reason I was interested in her at all was due to my mother being a suspect in her death.

"Yes, you would." He gave a succinct nod and then took a drink of his water as if to say *case closed*.

"Were they close, Babs and her mother?"

"What's this about?" Carl asked. "Are you here to discuss Babushka Tru, or are you here to discuss a book deal? I don't have time to waste."

"I was simply making conversation, Mr. Paxton. However, I don't want to waste your time. I'll pay for our lunch, take mine to go, and apologize for your inconvenience." I pushed my chair back.

"Aw, come on. Don't go off in a huff. Let's have our meal and talk about your book proposal. I didn't mean to be offensive. I'm just in the frame of mind that time is money."

I took a breath. "Well. . . . I suppose you *have* been under quite a bit of stress this week."

"You think? Babs wasn't just my client, she was . . . a friend."

"Right. Well, the book I'm proposing would be about my mother getting her start as a seamstress with Warner Brothers back in the seventies," I said. "She quickly moved up the ladder to the position of costuming assistant and then head costume designer before she started her own freelance career."

"Has she stepped on a lot of toes?" he asked.

"A few, I guess. Is that a problem?"

"The problem would be if she *hadn't*. Controversy sells. Without it, all you have is another boring book about an aging has-been."

My jaw dropped. "My mother is *not* an aging has-been!" This time I did walk out. I stopped by the counter and gave Blake enough money to cover the tab without waiting for a receipt.

"I didn't say she was!" Carl Paxton called after me.

I didn't look back. All I knew was that Carl Paxton and Babushka Tru had deserved each other. And from what I could see, he and Ms. Trublonski did too.

When I got back to the Seven-Year Stitch, I was mad enough to spit. Angus could tell right away, and he slunk off to his bed under the counter.

"It's not you, baby," I said in a soothing voice, but he wasn't buying it. He wouldn't be okay with me until my anger had abated. He wasn't taking any chances. It made me wonder if people had mistreated him before I rescued him from that puppy mill, or if it was merely a case of his being able to tell that something wasn't right and deciding to give me a wide berth until I was happy again.

Not ten minutes after I'd got back and took my little cardboard clock off the door, Sadie came in with my chicken salad croissant in a box.

"Here, sweetie," she said. "I didn't want you to starve."

"Thanks." My eyes glistened with unshed tears.

"Don't let him get to you. I don't know what he did or said, but—" She shook her head. "The guy seems slimy. He's certainly not worth crying over."

"I know. And it's not what he said so much, as how it ties in to what I've been concerned about," I said.

"Which is?"

"He said that without controversy, Mom's book—that I'm not even writing, you know—would be just another book from an aging has-been. And although I *know* Mom isn't a has-been, I'm afraid this mess will be the end of her career."

"But you know she's innocent," Sadie said. "Everything will be all right."

"I *do* know she's innocent, but this still might be enough to ruin her reputation."

"I see your point." She rubbed the back of her

neck. "Is there anyone else involved with the movie that you trust to give you more insight?"

"Maybe." I sighed. "I'll think about it."

"I gotta get back. It's the lunch rush. If you need me, though, call me."

"Thanks, Sadie!"

I took the croissant into my office. Angus decided he'd venture out for a bite of that. I tore off a piece and gave it to him as I checked my phone to see if I had the phone number for Ron Fitzpatrick, the director of photography. Luckily, I did.

"Hi, Ron," I said when he answered. "It's Marcy Singer."

"Marcy, hi. How've you been? I've been thinking about you and your mom. How's she doing?"

"We're both fine. We'll be glad when this whole mess is resolved, but we're doing okay," I said.

"Tell me about it," he said. "I don't even think poor Babs was murdered. I think she hit her head when she fell and that the local law enforcement is just trying to make a big deal out of nothing in order to get some publicity."

"Really? You don't think anyone did her in?"

He chuckled. "I think most of the people on the set wanted to kill her at least once—at least, the women did; she flirted with all us guys—but I don't think anyone really did it. In my opinion, she was wandering around where she shouldn't have been, and she stumbled. Case closed."

"Have the police questioned you?" I asked.

"Of course. They've talked to everybody who was on the set that day, as far as I know."

"That's a relief. I think Detectives Bailey and Ray tried to make Mom feel like she was public enemy number one."

Ron chuckled again. "Tell her welcome to the club, baby doll."

"So, playing devil's advocate and saying someone *did* push Babs, did you see anyone messing around where they shouldn't have been that morning?" I asked. "Was she arguing with anyone besides my mom?"

"Marcy, Babs was constantly arguing with somebody. Don't take this stuff to heart, okay?"

"I'm trying. I really am, but it's hard. I'm afraid these people are going to try to pin a murder on my mother," I said.

"Like I said, don't let them get to you. They're just trying to get her to say something to incriminate herself," he said.

"At least Babs' mother doesn't think Mom is guilty," I said, still fishing. "She came by the house night before last to ask Mom if she thought Babs might've committed suicide."

Ron scoffed. "As if. Babs loved herself too much for that."

"How about she and her mother?" I asked.

"Did they have a good relationship? I'm asking because Ms. Trublonski isn't wasting any time writing a tell-all book about Babs' life."

"I've never met Babs' mother, so I couldn't tell you anything about their relationship," he said. "But that's typical. Most of these people know they're in the capitalization business. If they don't move quickly on what they have to offer, someone else will step into their place."

"That's basically what Carl Paxton said."

"That loser?" Ron asked. "He's a snake. Don't trust that guy."

"Now that you mention it, he did have a certain reptilian quality about him," I said. "I only met him today, but it didn't take long to form an unfavorable opinion of him. What about Henry? Do you agree with his decision to continue making the movie?"

"It's not his decision," Ron said. "It's the decision of the backers. They have too much invested in it for everything to be flushed down the drain at this point. Besides, we were pretty early into filming, so we don't have that much that has to be redone. And the scenes that didn't feature Babs won't have to be refilmed at all."

"That's good. Still, it's a shame about the lost time and the lost footage," I said.

"Yeah, well. . . . The studio has already sold

clips of the movie—mainly behind-the-scenes stuff—to the networks. So we'll probably break even there."

Wow. Talk about your capitalization. . . .

For about an hour following lunch, I was half afraid Carl Paxton would stop by the Seven-Year Stitch to try to talk with me more about the fictitious book. That's why I was sitting on the sofa facing away from the window as I worked on my mauve pillowcase. I needn't have worried, though, because his time was valuable and couldn't be wasted, you know. Grrr. That man had made my skin crawl. I was glad I wasn't the only one who thought he was a creep.

I hadn't had a customer in over forty minutes, so I nearly jumped out of my skin when the bells over the door jingled. I was relieved to see that it was Mom and Alfred. Angus, who'd been lying at my feet, was delighted. I didn't know how he managed to run and wiggle at the same time.

Mom laughed as she cupped his big face in her hands. "Who's Grandma's pretty boy? Who is? Angus is! Yes, he is!"

Alfred rolled his eyes. "I never thought I'd live to see the day that Beverly Singer would call herself 'Grandma' to a dog."

"That makes two of us," I said. "But he's a special guy."

"He must be." Alfred sat beside me on the sofa and looked at my embroidery. "Nice."

"Thank you. So what have you two been up to?"

"We met with Henry." Mom sat on one of the red club chairs.

"And? Are you in or out?" I asked.

"I'm out."

"Oooh. Vera will hate that," I said.

Mom smiled. "Maybe she can work with Henry's new costume designer."

"What gives? Why aren't you going to do it?" I glanced around to make sure no one was about to come in. "Are you afraid Henry killed Babs?"

"It's not so much that," Alfred said. "Bev has decided that the pall Babushka's death has cast over the production has made it impossible to continue working on the film. She feels it's best to try to put this ordeal behind her with a new project."

"That's the press release version," Mom said. "Unofficially, I feel that until this mess is cleared up, I don't trust Henry and he doesn't trust me. We can't collaborate on a project if we don't trust each other. I might work with him again in the future, but not unless we feel at ease together again." She shrugged. "I might never be able to work with Henry Beaumont again . . . and vice versa."

"You see, your mother was designing the costumes seeing Babushka Tru as Sonam Zakaria," Alfred said. "Right now, she's unable to substitute another actress into the role."

"That's taking it too far, even for the press release," Mom told Alfred. "I'm a professional. I could design costumes for a donkey if that's who they put in the role. Stick with that first thing you said."

"I only want you to appear to be sympathetic in this," he said. "I want to make it seem as if you liked Ms. Tru."

"But I didn't," she said. "If you try to make people think I did, I'm going to look like a hypocrite. And I'm not. Besides, witnesses heard us arguing on the morning she died. The tabloids have already been going on about that."

"Still, Bev, people argue all the time, whether they like one another or not," Alfred said. "Didn't you like the girl at all?"

"No. Nobody did. I'm sorry she's dead, but it would be dishonest to say otherwise."

"What about Carl Paxton?" I asked Mom. "What do you know about him?"

"He's a cradle-robbing opportunist," she said.

"Do you think he might've killed Babs?" I asked.

"No. She was his meal ticket."

"I spoke with Ron Fitzpatrick a little while ago," I said. "He seems to think Babs wasn't murdered at all. He thinks she stumbled and fell."

"Maybe she did." Mom leaned forward. "Whatever happened, let it go, Marcella. It's not your business to investigate. Just stay out of it."

"I can't. You're my mother."

"That's why I'm telling you to stay out of it," she said. "You and I both need to stay out of this before we both get into more trouble than it's worth."

Chapter Sixteen

After Mom and Alfred left, I set up a three-way call with Vera and Reggie. Then I put my phone on speaker mode so I could work on my pillowcase while I talked. I'd finished one of them last night, and I was halfway through this one. I was fidgety when I was nervous, so having something to keep my hands busy was crucial to my well-being.

Reggie answered first. "Tallulah Falls Public Library, Reggie speaking."

"Hi, Reggie. It's Marcy. I'm also calling Vera, so we can all talk about the movie together. I promise it won't take long."

"We aren't too busy at the moment," she said. "We should be fine."

Vera answered, and I clued her in to what was going on.

"I just wanted to tell you both that Mom has

decided not to go forward with the movie," I said. "We both appreciate your willingness to help with the costumes, and I'm sorry you didn't get to see the project through to its completion."

"You said your Mom decided not to go forward," Vera said. "I heard Henry say in the press conference that he plans to continue work on the movie. Why doesn't your mother want to pursue it?"

I had to think about that one a second. I didn't want to tell Vera—and possibly Paul, by association—that Mom didn't trust Henry. I was afraid it would wind up in some newspaper that Mom was accusing Henry of murdering Babs. Whether she truly felt that way or not, we didn't need that piece of gossip showing up in a tabloid. I decided to fall back on Alfred's explanation.

"This whole ordeal has just been too much for her to handle," I said. "She wants to move on to something new and put this mess behind her as soon as possible."

"Can't say that I blame her there," Reggie said. "I was a little surprised that Henry is continuing on with the movie. I mean, I understand the movie has backers and they have a certain amount of influence, but Babushka Tru's death had to have impacted the entire cast and crew."

"I agree." I finished off a lazy daisy stitch and put a French knot in the center of another flower. "And I do think it will be several months before

Henry is able to move forward with the movie. The investigation will have to be completed, he'll have to hire a new lead, and he'll have to find another costume designer."

"Will the costumes your mother has already designed still be a part of the movie?" Vera asked.

"I'm not sure," I said. "I guess we'll have to wait and see. Again, I'm really sorry you didn't get to realize your dream of being a part of the movie and attending the premiere."

"Well, I'm not dead yet," Vera said. "And having a part in a movie is still on my bucket list. Henry might still want you and your chikankari expertise, Reggie. You should ask him."

"I don't think so," Reggie said. "If he is interested in having me continue working with the costumer, he'll let me know. I don't want to be pushy." She paused. "Plus, I kind of agree with Beverly—this movie is tainted now. I couldn't be a part of it without thinking of poor Babs every step of the way."

"Do you think they'll use Babs' death as a marketing draw?" Vera asked.

"They probably won't have to," I said. "People seem to always have a morbid curiosity. Besides, Ron Fitzpatrick, the director of photography, told me that they'd already released some behind-the-scenes footage to get some prerelease buzz going about the movie."

"I wonder if he shot anything the morning of Babs' death?" Reggie asked. "I'm sure the police have already asked him about it, but as a police chief's wife, it occurs to me that there might be something Ron captured that would shed some light on what happened to Babs."

"You're right, Reggie," I said. "I never even thought of that. I'll have to call Ron back and ask him. Thanks for the tip."

"I'll also check with Paul to see if he has access to the footage," Vera said. "If Ron sent it out over the AP wire, then I'm sure he does."

"Thanks, guys," I said.

By the time we'd finished up our conversation, I'd completed another large portion of the pillowcase and had decided I needed to talk with Ron some more. But first, I needed to stretch. I got Angus's leash from behind the counter, locked the door, and took him for a walk up the street. We walked all the way up to the town square where the black wrought-iron clock stood.

I'd just noticed that the clock read three twenty-five when I heard someone calling my name. I turned to see Carl Paxton coming my way.

"You're away from your shop quite a bit for someone trying to maintain a business, aren't you?" he asked.

"And you're awfully dense for someone who should be able to take a hint." I felt Angus stiffen at my side. "I thought leaving before we'd had lunch today should have clued you in to the fact that I don't have anything else to say to you."

"Yes, well . . . I wanted to come back and thank you for lunch. Despite the lack of companionship while dining, the salad was delicious. I'm sorry you took what I said to you as an insult. It wasn't meant to be."

"Nevertheless, you have to admit, it wasn't flattering," I said.

"Agreed, but it was the truth. I did have a chance to call some of my contacts, and they're interested in a book on your mother's Hollywood experiences."

"That's great. I need to get back. Would you like to walk with me back to the shop?"

"Of course," he said.

We walked back down the street, which proved to be a daunting task for me because I was trying to keep Angus from snuffling Carl. It was apparent to Angus that I wasn't comfortable and was, in fact, a bit irritated by Carl's presence, so he was trying to get over to the man to check him out and form his own opinion.

"The key to whether or not my contacts are interested in the book is content," Carl said as I unlocked the door.

"Naturally," I said. "Are you talking photographs? Mom has plenty of those."

"Photographs are nice, of course, but it's the controversy that will sell. People want to read juicy gossip." He walked over to the counter and leaned against it nonchalantly. "Take her dislike for Babushka Tru, for example. Some venomous comments on the young starlet would be a good start."

I gaped at the man until I felt like an idiot and closed my mouth. Then I counted to three and said, "Babs was your client. Her mother *is* your client. Why would you want my mother to say something nasty about Babs in her book?"

"Three reasons—because Babs *was* my client, because her mother *is* my client, and because your mother *will be* my client," he said. "Publicized fighting between the two living clients would mean increased book sales for both. It's a win-win."

Before I could respond, Ted walked into the shop. He looked from me to Angus, who was still on his leash and standing slightly in front of me and between Carl and me. "Is there a problem here?"

"Um, no . . . not really," I said. "Ted, this is Carl Paxton, Babushka Tru's manager. Carl, this is Detective Ted Nash."

"Pleasure to meet you, Detective," Carl said. He raised an eyebrow at me. "Are there normally problems here, or do Ms. Singer's friends share her propensity for overreacting?"

Ted placed his hands on his waist. "I don't know why you're here, but I think it's time for you to leave."

"Yes, I suppose you're right," he said. "Ms. Singer, you have my number. Should you decide there's enough vitriol in your mother's recollections to make them worthwhile for the rest of us, please give me a call." He nodded at both Ted and me. "Good afternoon."

As soon as Carl left, I unleashed Angus and sank against Ted. "Man, am I glad to see you."

"What was that creep doing here?"

I gave him an abbreviated version of my excuse for talking with Carl, my walking out on Carl at lunch, and then him locating me in the town square. "I guess I was hoping talking to him could provide me some information on Ms. Trublonski or Babs . . . something that would absolutely clear my mother of any wrongdoing."

He kissed the top of my head and then walked me over to the sofa. Angus stayed right on our heels, although he kept an eye on the door to make sure Carl wasn't coming back.

As we sat on the sofa facing away from the window, I blew out a breath. "It's sad, really. Babs had been Paxton's client for all those years, but it seems she wasn't important to him at all as a person. He doesn't seem upset about her death. He's convinced Ms. Trublonski to move forward with a tell-all book about Babs' life, and he even agreed to represent Mom in a book deal if, basically, she'd trash Babs, among other stars."

"That's not Bev's style," Ted said. "Even in the short amount of time I've known her, I can't imagine her writing a book just to profit from spreading malicious gossip about someone else."

"You're right. I don't really know what I was hoping to find out from Carl anyway. I don't know how often he visited the set, if ever."

"I'm not trying to be a buttinsky, but you and your mom need to sit down and have a heart-to-heart," he said. "Whether she wants to or not, she needs to talk with you and tell you what she either knows or thinks she knows."

"I agree. She and Alfred came by here earlier today. She told me that she isn't going to continue working on the film because she doesn't trust Henry." I placed Angus's leash on the coffee table. "I told her I'd spoken with Ron, the photography director, and that he thinks Babs might've simply fell on her own, hitting her head and causing the blunt-force trauma herself."

"What did she think of that idea?"

"She said she doesn't know what happened but that I need to stay out of it." I looked up at Ted to gauge his reaction. Her advice sounded almost identical to some Ted had given me in the past.

He rubbed the back of his neck. "I'm inclined to

agree with her, but the fact that she said it makes me think she knows more than she's saying. I believe you should find out what she knows, and then pass it along to me so I can look into it."

I smiled. "Thank you. You're wonderful."

Ted gave me a slow, lazy smile. "Prove it."

I gave him a kiss that thoroughly supported my opinion.

Before Ted returned to work, we decided that I'd talk Mom into agreeing that the three of us would go out to dinner that evening in Lincoln City since I didn't have a class. He'd give me plenty of time to go home and talk with Mom, and then she and I would get ready for dinner, and he'd pick us up. After we returned home, Ted and I could sit on the porch in the moonlight, and I could tell him what I'd discovered.

As soon as Ted left, I called Mom. She answered on the first ring, but she sounded cautious.

"Hey," I said in my brightest voice. "Ted is taking us out to dinner tonight in Lincoln City. Won't that be fun?"

"Oh, honey, I don't think I'd be much company this evening."

"Nonsense. You have to eat, and Ted and I aren't *company*. We're family," I said.

"Hmmm . . . an interesting choice of words," she said. "In that case, I guess I'd better go along."

I debated on telling her not to read too much

into what I'd said, but since she'd agreed to go, I decided not to press my luck. "Great. Angus and I will be home shortly after five o'clock. I think Ted is going to pick us up around seven."

"All right, darling. See you then."

Good. Mission accomplished. And since I'd almost accomplished another mission—the set of mauve pillowcases—I searched the shelves for another project to do. I found a beautiful stamped cross-stitch kit that replicated one of Monet's prints. I decided to embroider the print for Mom . . . to show her that something good could come out of the adversity we were currently facing.

Angus and I got home at about fifteen minutes past five. I didn't see Mom anywhere, so I called to tell her we were home.

"I'll be down in a few!" she called.

I went ahead and fed Angus, and then went into the living room to wait for Mom. I picked up the remote, switched on the television, and curled up in the chair. The local news was on.

I nearly nodded off listening to the droning voices of the news anchors until I heard a deep male voice say, " . . . released this footage of Babushka Tru as Bollywood star Sonam Zakaria."

My eyes popped open, and I sat up straighter.

In the film clip, Babs was doing a scene from the movie. Then Henry yelled "cut," but the camera kept rolling to get the behind-the-scenes coverage Ron had mentioned. Babs looked to someone off camera and winked. Then she giggled. When she noticed Henry and the male lead watching, she turned and flounced away in the opposite direction.

Did Babs have a boyfriend on the set? Had it been Carl Paxton she was flirting with? It had certainly not been Henry.

Mom came downstairs, and Angus greeted her at the landing.

"Has he already eaten?" she asked. "Would you like me to put him out for a few minutes before we leave?"

"Sure," I said. I turned and saw that she'd already gotten dressed for dinner. She was wearing gray slacks and an ivory silk blouse. "No, wait. Let me get him. He might get your clothes dirty."

I went to the back door, opened it, and called for Angus. He loped through the kitchen and into the yard.

"You look great," I told Mom.

"Thank you," she said. "I've decided I'm going to try to start putting this disaster behind me. I'm going to enjoy dinner tonight, and I'm not going to think about Babushka Tru or Henry or the movie or any of it."

I pressed my lips together.

"What?" she asked. "You're not okay with that?"

"I am," I said. "Just, I think we should talk before you stop thinking about it. And then maybe we can *both* stop thinking about it."

She headed back toward the living room. "What do you want to know?"

"First off, I want to know whether or not you believe Henry killed Babs," I said, resuming my spot on the chair and shutting off the television. "I've never known you to drop out of a movie before, and you've admitted it's because you don't trust Henry. If you have evidence that could help the police, you need to tell them."

"I don't have any evidence, Marcella." Mom sat on the sofa. "I don't really even believe Henry killed that girl. I don't *know* that he didn't, but I don't think he did. What bugs me to my very soul about Henry is that I thought he was one of the good guys." She looked down at her hands. "In Hollywood, you find that a lot of people have their own moral codes—or, rather, their own immoral codes. Henry wasn't like that. He was a stand-up guy . . . always doing the right thing, always faithful to his wife of thirty years. . . . At least, that's what I believed until I found out Babs was pregnant and started investigating the rumors that he was having an affair with her."

"Well, they *were* just rumors," I said. "You've

said yourself that things aren't always what they appear in La La Land."

"I know, but when I saw him hugging up to her in those photographs and then remembered how he'd told me to get along with her no matter what. . . ." She shook her head. "He was in love with her, Marcella. He adored her. I've known Henry and his wife, Eileen, for years. Eileen is devoted to Henry, and I'd always thought he was devoted to her too. I feel I don't even know Henry Beaumont anymore. And that's why I can't work with him."

"Did you tell him that?"

"Of course not," she said. "We gave him Alfred's response. And what Alfred came up with is true—this trauma has affected me deeply. Only, it's the trauma of losing the man I believed Henry Beaumont to be—not the death of Babushka Tru."

"I'm sorry, Mom." I wanted to dig deeper—ask her if Babs had been flirting with someone on the set, find out if Henry was jealous, see what other cast and crew members thought of Babs, Henry, and Carl Paxton—but it didn't seem to be the right time. She'd opened her heart to me, and I could see how badly she was hurting over Henry. Now she wanted to put all talk of the movie and Babs' murder behind her and enjoy her evening, and I wasn't going to deny her that.

Chapter Seventeen

The three of us were relatively quiet as we drove to Lincoln City to the seafood restaurant where Ted had made reservations. I made a couple halfhearted attempts at conversation, but then I gave up. Finally, Ted saved the day—or, at least, the trip to Lincoln City.

"Marcy, you know Manu and I went to investigate the primary crime scene where the gunman's body was found, right?" he asked.

"Yes, the place where Vera found the button," I said.

"Yeah, the infamous button which had probably been there for ten years." He laughed slightly. "Don't get me wrong. We did ask around about it, but it didn't seem to mean anything to anyone at the office."

"Did you find anything else of any importance?" I asked.

He shook his head. "The place has been trampled all to pieces. Thank goodness, we did a thorough search before the movie people got there. No offense, Bev."

"None taken," she said. "Tell me more about this gunman and why you're so desperate to find his partner."

"Well, for one thing, we're pretty sure his partner is also his killer," Ted said. "And while the young man who shot at me turned out to be a computer expert, his partner was likely the mastermind behind the entire operation. He can find another hacker. He's the one we need to shut down. He's the one who's truly dangerous."

"Hey, the hacker was dangerous enough for me," I said. "He shot at you!"

"Yeah, but he missed." Ted grinned.

"It's not funny," I said.

"I know. But it's behind us now," he said. "Let's move past it. Speaking of moving on, Bev, what are your plans now that you've decided to drop out of Henry's movie?"

"I don't know yet," she said. "I might take a little time off before taking on a new project. This ordeal has really hurt me, and I need to heal."

Her voice broke slightly, and I quickly began to talk about some new crewel embroidery kits I'd ordered. I hated for her to be so upset. I knew then that I was going to give Henry Beaumont a piece of my mind.

I set my alarm to wake me up early Friday morning. When it buzzed, I quickly shut it off and quietly took a bath and got dressed. I definitely didn't want to wake up Mom.

I fed Angus and ate a granola bar, and then I took Angus for a walk around the neighborhood. It was rainy, and I didn't want to leave him in the backyard. I wrote Mom a note telling her that Angus had been fed and walked but that she might want to walk him again when she got up. I told her I had an errand to run and was leaving early. I told her to call me if she needed anything.

And then I went to Henry Beaumont's hotel. I didn't want to catch him completely off guard, so I called from the lobby and asked if I could come up. He said yes.

When I got to the room, he opened the door in his bathrobe. His hair was wet, and it was apparent he'd taken a shower just before I'd phoned. He held up his right index finger to let me know he'd be with me in a minute, and I saw that he was holding his cell phone to his ear with left hand.

"Yes, angel. I love you, too. I'm looking forward

to seeing you tomorrow." He ended the call and apologized for his appearance. "I'm sorry I didn't have a chance to get dressed before you got up here. Eileen called right after you did. If you'll excuse me, I'll put on some clothes."

"Okay." I looked around the room as Henry stepped into the bathroom and shut the door. The bed was a wreck. He'd done some tossing and turning last night. Judging by the dark circles under his eyes, he didn't get much sleep either.

He emerged from the bathroom in khaki slacks, a blue polo shirt, and his wet hair combed. He was still barefoot, but he sat down on the bed to put on his socks and shoes. "What can I do for you, Marcy? Your mother made it plain to me yesterday that she was finished with me."

"That's what I'm here to talk with you about." I sat on the undisturbed bed across from him. "She is so hurt, Henry. She thought you were a topnotch person . . . a gentleman . . . a man among men."

"And now she believes me to be a murderer?"

"No. She thinks you were the father of Babushka Tru's unborn child," I said.

He closed his eyes. "Nothing could be farther from the truth."

"Did you love Babs?" I asked.

"Very much." He opened his eyes, and they were swimming with tears. "She was my daughter."

I sat there like an idiot, simply staring at him.

"I only found out a few months ago," he said. "One night many years ago, Mita Trublonski and I hooked up at a party. We'd both been drinking . . . a lot . . . and she wound up pregnant. She didn't tell me."

"Why on earth not?"

He shrugged. "I made it obvious to her the next morning that what we'd done had been a mistake. I went home and begged Eileen for forgiveness. She forgave me, and the scandal never even hit the newspapers. It would've been bad for Mita and me, but it would've been even worse for our spouses. It meant nothing . . . and yet it meant everything."

"Was Mita sure Babs belonged to you and not to her husband?" I asked.

"Yes, because her husband had left her two weeks prior to that night, and they hadn't been sleeping together for months," he said. "When I found out, I couldn't wait to get to know Babs. I bought the entire series of *Surf Dad* and watched them over and over just to see my little girl growing up. I went through back issues of magazines, downloaded videos from the Internet. . . ."

"And you developed this movie project for her."

"Yeah," he whispered.

"Did she know?" I asked.

He shook his head and snatched a tissue from the box on the nightstand. "No. Mita and I decided not to tell her until she'd made her comeback. We didn't want her to think she succeeded only because she was my daughter. We wanted her to do it on her own. And then we'd tell her." He wiped his nose on the tissue.

I thought back to the photos I'd seen of Henry cuddling Babs. I supposed it could have been fatherly affection I'd been seeing. "But you were so indulgent toward her. Didn't she find that odd?"

"No. She knew I loved her. I told her she was like the daughter I never had. Which was true." A tear dripped off his chin and he flicked at it with the tissue. "Eileen couldn't have children."

"How did she feel when she learned about Babs?"

"She was hurt, but she was happy too. I think she thought this might be a way for her to finally get the child she'd always wanted." He groaned. "Why didn't we ever adopt? We talked about it so often, but we never did anything about it. Now it's too late. And the one child I have . . . *had* . . . is gone."

"It's not too late to adopt," I said. "There are plenty of children out there who need good homes."

He nodded and continued to weep.

I got up and moved to the other bed so I could

put my arm around him. "I'm sorry, Henry. I'm so sorry. I had no idea."

"Mom, you were wrong about Henry," I told her when she answered the phone. I was cradling the phone between my ear and shoulder as I unlocked the door to the Seven-Year Stitch.

"Marcella, please tell me you didn't go talk with that man." The exasperation was evident in her voice.

"I did, and I'm glad I did." I opened the door, slipped my keys into my jeans pocket, and took my phone—much to the relief of my neck and shoulder. "He wasn't in love with Babs. He was her father."

I placed my tote bag and purse behind the counter. Mom was so quiet that at first I was afraid I'd disconnected her with my machinations at the front door. "Mom? You there?"

"I'm here," she said softly. "Did you say that Henry was Babs' father?"

"Yes." I explained how Henry and Mita Trublonski had a one-night stand many years ago that resulted in Babs. I also told Mom that Mita had decided not to tell Henry until recently because she didn't want to destroy their respective families.

"Then why did she suddenly come forward?" Mom asked.

"Henry really didn't go into detail about that, but I'm thinking Babs needed a comeback and Mita thought it would be a good time for Babs' father, the producer, to find out about her paternity."

"Did he get a blood test?" she asked. "Mita could've been lying, you know."

"Look, Mom, all I know is that Henry believes he was Babs' father and that he's devastated over her death. He told me that he and Eileen couldn't have children and that he was thrilled to learn he had a daughter."

"How did Eileen feel about that?"

"He said she was angry and hurt at first but that she'd made peace with it," I said. "He'd spoken with her on the phone before I'd arrived, and he said she was coming to be with him tomorrow."

"I need to talk with him," Mom said. "I need to make things right between us. I don't know that I'll go back on my decision to drop out of this movie, but I've got to support Henry. Thanks for getting to the bottom of his relationship with Babs. I should've done like you and asked him point-blank rather than jumping to conclusions. I knew Henry was a better man than that."

"Well, still, he *did* have an affair that led to Babs," I said.

"Maybe. And maybe Mita was just jerking his

chain. I'm going to hang up and call him now. I'll talk with you later, darling. Thanks again for letting me know."

I was humming a little tune as I dusted the merchandise area of the shop and refilled the yarn and floss bins with stock from the storeroom. Things were looking up. I felt sure Babs' murder investigation would soon be concluded.

I sat down in the sit-and-stitch square and opened up the Monet print kit. This would be a beautiful piece once it was completed and framed.

I had no idea what evidence the Tallulah County Police Department had, but there was obviously nothing that could conclusively point to Mom or to anyone else in the cast or crew, or else the police would have made an arrest already. We were definitely coming through the other side of the tunnel at last.

Ted stopped by with lunch—chef's salads from MacKenzies' Mochas—at about one o'clock.

"Where's the fur ball?" he asked when he noticed Angus was conspicuously absent.

"He stayed home with Mom this morning," I said. "I had an errand to run and didn't think he'd be welcome to tag along."

He arched a brow. "An errand, Inch-High Private Eye?"

I grinned. "Okay, so I might have been doing a *little* detecting. I went to talk with Henry Beaumont."

"About?"

"You saw how upset Mom was last night, and I went to tell him about it." I put the clock on the door and then got us some sodas from the minifridge in my office. "But it turns out, she was entirely wrong about him. He wasn't an old lothario after all. He was a young . . . okay, not so young . . . he was . . . what? A middle-aged. . . ."

"Marcy."

"He was Babs' dad!" I spurted. "Can you believe it? Apparently, he and Mita had a tryst all these years ago, and he's Babs' father. Only Mom thinks Mita might have been lying to Henry in order to get Babs a part in one of Henry's movies, so she was going to call Henry and tell him she was sorry she misjudged him and to see whether or not he got a paternity test before he just took Mita's word for everything. I'm sure he did, though, aren't you? I mean, of course, he'd check out the story. How convenient for— "

Ted silenced me with a kiss. Afterward, he told me I'd gotten so carried away with my story that he was afraid I'd hyperventilate.

"Thank you so much, then, for coming to my rescue," I said. "The kiss was much better than having me breathe into a paper bag. But I really do think everything is going to be all right now, don't you?"

He nodded, but I know him well enough to know that it was an insincere nod.

"You don't think so," I said. "Why don't you think so?"

"There's still a murderer out there, Marce. Things won't really be better until he's caught."

"But is the Tallulah County Police Department even *positive* that Babs was murdered?" I asked. "Ron Fitzpatrick seems to think she stumbled and fell on her own—no blow to the head, no push, no nothing except her own clumsiness."

"I'm afraid not, Inch-High. There was solid evidence that Babs was struck on the back of the head with a blunt object and that she couldn't have obtained the injury in the fall."

I huffed. "Okay, what about Carl Paxton? Now that we're sure Henry and Babs weren't having an affair, he's bound to have been the father of Babs' baby. Have the police talked with him?"

"I don't know. I'm with the Tallulah Falls Sheriff's Department, remember? Anything the TCPD shares with us, they do as an interdepartmental courtesy," he said. He studied my face for a second. "But I'll check into it and see what I can find out."

I smiled. "Thanks."

He held up a hand. "But, you need to stop

jumping to conclusions. One, the TCPD hasn't yet determined the paternity of Babs' child. Two, Henry could've been lying or lied to about Babs being his daughter. And three, Ron could've told you he thinks Babs simply slipped and fell because that's what he wants you to think ... or maybe that's what *he* wants to think. You have to play devil's advocate and look at the entire picture, babe."

"I don't. *You* do. That's why they pay you the big bucks." I winked and popped a crouton into my mouth.

"Oh, yeah. That's the only reason you're dating me, isn't it? My mansion and my Ferrari are real turn-ons."

I laughed. "You're the turn-on, Ted Nash. You don't need any fancy trappings."

"It's a good thing."

My phone rang, and I saw that it was Mom. "I'd better take this just to make sure she's okay." I pressed the answer button. "Hey, Mom. What's up?"

"I don't know that to do," she said.

"What's wrong? Are you crying?" I asked.

"He's dead. Henry's dead." Her words ended on a sob.

"Mom, calm down. What do you mean he's dead?" I put the phone on speaker so Ted could hear too.

"After we spoke on the phone this morning, I told him I'd buy him a coffee," she said. "We thought it would do us both good. But when I got here, the door to his room was ajar. He's dead."

"Beverly, it's Ted. Did you touch anything?"

"Just Henry," she said. "I put my purse down and patted his face. I thought he'd fainted. When he didn't come to, I took his pulse."

"Hold tight," Ted said. "And don't touch anything. I'm on my way."

"I'm going with you," I said.

He didn't argue as I turned out the lights and locked the door. Instead, he called Manu and asked him to meet us at Henry's hotel. Since the hotel was in Tallulah County rather than in the town of Tallulah Falls, he also called Detective Bailey and asked him and Detective Ray to come to the hotel as well. I wasn't looking forward to seeing Detectives Bailey and Ray again . . . especially since my fingerprints were all over Henry's hotel room and my mother had found his body.

Chapter Eighteen

I was relieved to see Manu's white Bronco in the parking lot of Henry's hotel when we arrived. The pit of dread that had been gnawing at my stomach returned almost immediately, however, as I heard sirens blaring nearer and nearer.

"So much about keeping this quiet from the press until there's some sort of official word," I muttered.

As Ted and I approached the front doors of the hotel, Detectives Ray and Bailey—along with two additional cars of law enforcement personnel—roared up to the loading area and screeched to a halt.

"Hold it right there!" Detective Bailey yelled from the passenger side window. "Don't move until I get out of this car!"

Ted stiffened and placed a protective hand at the small of my back.

Detective Bailey put up his window and got out of the car. "What do you think you're doing here? Neither of you have any business here. This is not your jurisdiction, Nash, and you certainly don't have any reason to be here, Ms. Singer."

"First off, this is a public place," Ted said. "No one has officially confirmed that Henry Beaumont is even dead." He nodded to the cars in which uniformed officers and plainclothes officers still sat. "Won't you feel ridiculous if it turns out that Henry Beaumont was just passed out?"

"You said her mother—the same woman who we believe to be the last person to see Babushka Trublonski alive—thought Henry was dead," Detective Bailey said. "I'm figuring she should know."

"All right," said Detective Ray, joining our happy little trio. "Let's go upstairs and see what we've got." He called for the other two carloads of police officers to stand by.

The four of us went upstairs to Henry Beaumont's room. Detective Ray knocked on the door. Manu opened it.

I could see Mom sobbing into a fist in a chair in the corner, so I brushed past Detective Ray to go kneel in front of her.

"Mom, are you all right?" I asked.

"No. How could I possibly be all right? Henry's dead. I'd behaved so badly toward him over this whole Babs incident, and now he's gone."

"Out!" Detective Bailey bellowed. "The two of you need to get out of this room immediately. Nash, take them to the seating area out in front of the elevators for now. We'll be by to talk with them in a minute."

I could tell from the muscle in Ted's jaw that he was clenching his teeth, but he didn't say anything. After all, what *could* he say? Detective Bailey was right. Mom and I shouldn't be in the room if it was potentially a crime scene. And from the scrap of conversation I'd caught between Manu and the detectives, Henry had definitely not passed out. He was dead.

As Ted led Mom and me to the seating area, I heard Detective Ray barking orders.

"Crime scene, I want you people sweeping this room," he said. "Bag everything! You two, go down to the front desk. I want this floor secured so that no unauthorized persons come up here. I don't want this crime scene turned into a media circus. And get the security footage of the lobby and this floor from six this morning until now!"

The two uniformed officers rushed past, bypassed the elevators, and ran down the stairs. I could hear their heavy steps echoing as the door slammed shut.

The seating area was comprised of a brown leather sofa, two matching chairs, and end tables on either side of the sofa. Mom and I sat on the sofa, while Ted took an armchair with his back to the wall so he could see what was going on in the hallway outside Henry's room. None of us said anything.

It wasn't but a few minutes until Manu joined us. He sat in the chair beside Ted and, in hushed tones, told us that Detectives Bailey and Ray had asked him what he'd found upon arriving.

"I told them that when I got here, Ms. Singer opened the door and let me in," he said. "She was in obvious distress and said she believed Mr. Beaumont to be dead. I checked his pulse and found it to be nonexistent."

"What about time of death?" Ted asked.

"As you know, the medical examiner will only be able to narrow the time frame down to a few hours here at the scene." I knew Manu was saying that for Mom's and my benefit, rather than for Ted's. "But one of the first things the crime scene techs bagged was Beaumont's phone. Seeing what time he last made or received a call could be the easiest way to further estimate the time of death prior to autopsy."

"Did you see any wounds?" Ted asked.

Manu shook his head. "Nothing. And I didn't see a murder weapon either."

"Then it's possible Henry had a heart attack or something," Mom said, her voice sounding hopeful. I understood her feelings. How much better it would be if Henry's heart simply gave out as opposed to his being murdered.

"Anything's possible," Manu said, but he didn't sound very convincing . . . at least, not to me.

The foregone conclusion in everyone's mind—well, except Mom's maybe—was that the same person who'd killed Babushka Tru had murdered Henry Beaumont. Who, why, and how were the only questions the rest of us, including Detectives Bailey and Ray, were asking ourselves.

After about thirty minutes, Detective Ray came out and asked Mom and me to come to the police station with him to answer some questions.

"I'll drive them," Ted said.

"You need anything else from me?" Manu asked.

"No, Manu, but I appreciate your hanging around," Detective Ray said. "If I have any more questions, I'll call you." He turned back to Ted, Mom and me. "We'll meet you at the station."

On the way to the police station, I'd called Alfred. He'd told me he'd contact Cam Whitting and that one or both of them would be at the police station as soon as possible.

"Do not let your mother answer any questions," he'd warned me.

Now I was sitting in an interrogation room

with Detective Ray, staring at the huge gray caterpillars that were his eyebrows as he turned on
a recording device. I knew Ted was in the obser-
vation room—he'd not been allowed to be with
me as I was questioned, of course. But knowing
he was there was a comfort. Also, being inter-
viewed by Detective Ray rather than Detective
Bailey was a comfort. I don't know why Bailey
had so much animosity toward me. Or maybe he
and Detective Ray simply did the good-cop-bad-
cop routine, and Bailey had the bad-cop role down
pat.

Detective Ray recited my rights, told me I
wasn't under arrest, and was under no obligation
to answer his questions, and then he asked me
those questions.

"Why did you go see Henry Beaumont this
morning?" he asked.

That was a good question. I couldn't very well
say that I'd gone to give the man a piece of my
mind. "My mom was so upset because she believed
Henry and Babs had been having an affair. She'd
worked with Henry for years, and I hated to see
their relationship—both personal and professional—
go down the drain. I went to Henry to get the truth."

"And what did he tell you?"

"He told me that Babs was his biological daughter," I said. "He didn't know it until recently—

before he began shooting the picture—but he and Mita, Babs' mother, had decided not to tell Babs yet."

"That's quite a revelation," said Detective Ray. "Why would he share it with you if he and the girl's mother were keeping it quiet?"

I shrugged. "I suppose that with Babs dead, it didn't matter who knew anymore. Henry's wife knew, and though she'd been hurt in the beginning, she'd made peace with it. Henry had been hoping to build a relationship with his daughter. He and Eileen, his wife, have no children, so to find Babs and then lose her in such a short amount of time was devastating to him."

"Is that how he appeared to you this morning?" he asked. "Devastated?"

"Yes. He was very distraught," I said. "He seemed glad that his wife was coming to join him tomorrow. Wait. Has anyone contacted her yet?"

Detective Ray nodded. "We've alerted police officers in her area, and they're probably meeting with her now."

"The poor thing. . . . I'm so sorry for her."

"Did Mr. Beaumont say anything else to you while you were there this morning?" he asked. "Did he tell you who he suspected in the murder of his daughter?"

"No, he didn't. We didn't talk about the fact

that she'd been murdered," I said. "We only spoke about the sad reality of her death."

"How did Mr. Beaumont seem when you left him?"

"He was sad. He was crying. I hugged him before I left, and then as soon as I got to the Seven-Year Stitch, I called Mom. I thought she needed to know the truth and make peace with Henry."

"Make peace?" The giant caterpillars leapt toward Detective Ray's hairline.

"That was a bad choice of words," I said quickly. "I knew she'd misjudged Henry by thinking he was having an affair with Babs, and she'd refused to work with him on the film any longer, and I. . . ." I glanced at the two-way mirror in desperation. Of course, I couldn't see Ted, but I was grasping for anything that *wouldn't* be condemning to my mother. "I just wanted her to know the truth. I wanted her to comfort him and to let him know she was there for him."

"What was her reaction to your news?" Detective Ray asked.

I asked myself what Ted would say to me if he could whisper in my ear right now. He'd tell me not to babble . . . to answer the questions succinctly and then stop talking. So I said, "She was supportive."

"She wasn't surprised?" he asked.

"I believe she was, but she was also relieved.

She said she knew Henry was a better man than to have an affair with a young starlet," I said.

"Did she mention going to see him?"

"She said she was going to call him." I then pointed out that they had Henry's cell phone and could confirm the call.

He smiled slightly. "We did confirm the call. When did you discover that your mother had gone to visit Mr. Beaumont at his hotel room?"

"When she called and told me that she found him lying unconscious in his room."

"To your knowledge, were your mother and Mr. Beaumont having an affair?" Detective Ray asked.

"Certainly not! Mom was friends with both Henry *and* his wife," I said. "That's why she'd been upset when she thought he'd been having an affair with Babs."

"Are you sure that's the only reason? After all, they did meet in his hotel room."

"Yes," I said through gritted teeth. "I'm sure my mother was not romantically involved with Henry Beaumont."

Detective Ray smiled. "Okay."

Okay? That's it? Okay? Of course, I didn't say that. I just thought it . . . vehemently. "Is that all?"

"For now," he said. "Thank you for your cooperation."

I refused to tell him he was welcome. Instead, I

scraped my chair across the floor and stood. Detective Ray walked to the door and opened it for me. I went through it and was glad to see that Ted was waiting for me in the hall.

"Do you have the hotel's security footage yet?" Ted asked Detective Ray.

"Yes."

"May we see it?"

Detective Ray frowned up at Ted, who was a good head taller than he. "Why?"

"Well, Beverly and Marcy are familiar with the cast and crew of the movie Henry Beaumont had been working on," Ted said. "Someone might slip under your radar, but they might recognize him or her as a potential suspect."

The older man pursed his lips. "Good point. When Bailey's finished with Ms. Singer, I'll have him let us know and we'll all go to the viewing room together."

"Thanks," Ted said.

"Thank *you*," I told Ted as soon as Detective Ray was out of earshot. "I hadn't even thought of that."

He inclined his head. "It's apparent that they think they've already got their suspect, but if you or your mom could recognize anyone else who'd come to see Henry this morning, it'll at least give them another person they'll have to investigate."

I rested my head on his chest. "You're wonderful."

"Don't flatter me yet," he said. "You might not recognize anyone."

"Even if we don't, you're wonderful."

It was a packed viewing room. In addition to Ted, Mom, me, Detective Ray and Detective Bailey, Alfred and Cam were there. Plus, the audiovisual guy. We were all crowded around one computer monitor watching hour after hour of people coming into the lobby. The AV guy did fast-forward it, slowing down or going back only if we saw someone we thought was familiar.

We saw the mail carrier arrive, people checking in and out, and employees arriving at, as well as leaving from, the hotel. Of course, we saw me, but that was old news to the detectives. I was stifling a yawn when something caught my eye.

"Stop," I said. "Go back and run it at regular speed."

The AV guy, whose name I think was Marshall Feldman, did as I'd asked. "Need it any slower?"

"Can you do that?" I asked.

"Sure." He ran the footage forward in slow motion.

"Isn't that Sonny Carlisle, the locations manager?" I asked Mom.

"Yes, but he's staying at the same hotel," she said.

"Still, I think we need to see if any of the movie people we see in the lobby turn up at Henry's door," I said.

"She's right," Ted agreed.

Detective Ray wrote *S. Carlisle* on the notepad in front of him. "Any other movie folks you see, point them out."

In addition to Sonny, we saw Ron Fitzpatrick and a makeup artist and a cameraman Mom had recognized. Hers had been the last familiar face we'd seen.

The AV guy then called up the security footage of Henry's floor. Sonny had gone to Henry's room, had been let in, and had stayed for about fifteen minutes. His visit had taken place between the time that I'd left and that Mom had arrived. Before Sonny had arrived, a TCPD officer had been to Henry's room; but other than Mom, no one had been into the room after Sonny had left.

I felt a chill. Could Sonny have killed Henry?

Chapter Nineteen

When we got home from the police station, I let Angus out into the backyard—he'd had to stay inside entirely too long—and then I called and ordered a pizza. I knew neither Mom nor I had any desire to cook.

Ted took three sodas from the fridge and set them on the table. "Let's talk."

We sat down around the table and opened our sodas. Ted took out his notepad.

"I want to approach this as if I were investigating Henry's death," he said. "That way, I can get a better idea of what happened to Henry as well as what the TCPD believe happened."

Mom nodded, slightly frowning, but I knew exactly what Ted meant. The Tallulah County Police Department was looking hard at Mom as a suspect in Henry's death, and Ted wanted to help her by figuring out what the investigators were thinking. He and I both knew—without coming right out and saying so—that Detectives Bailey and Ray wouldn't want Ted having any information about this case at all. As had happened on one other occasion of which I was personally aware, Ted was too close to the suspect to be considered impartial. They'd definitely shut him out, and they'd share as little information as possible with Manu. Whatever we found out, we'd have to learn on our own.

"Beverly, tell me exactly what happened when you arrived at the hotel," Ted said.

"Okay. I went into the lobby and straight to the elevators," she said.

"Did you see anyone acting strangely?" he asked. "Did anyone seem to be in a particular hurry to exit the building?"

Mom shook her head. "No, not really."

"Okay. So you go up in the elevator. Were you the only one in the elevator, or were others in the car?"

"I was alone," she said. "I stepped out when I got to Henry's floor, and I went to his room. I was surprised to find that the door wasn't pulled up all the way. Still, I knocked, but Henry didn't answer."

"And when he didn't answer, you went on inside?" Ted asked.

"Yes. As I said, the door wasn't completely closed, so I pushed it open." She closed her eyes and winced. "Poor Henry. . . . He was lying there on the floor."

"Tell me what else you saw when you opened the door," he prompted. "Was the bed still unmade? Were there any dishes around? Did anything strike you as being unusual or out of place?"

Mom looked up at the ceiling and considered his questions. "The bed hadn't been made, but other than that, the room was tidy. He'd apparently had breakfast brought up to his room because the tray and dishes were sitting on the table by the window." She met Ted's inquisitive gaze. "Nothing struck me as odd . . . other than the fact that Henry was unconscious on the floor."

"Did you see any apparent cause of death?" Ted asked.

She shook her head.

"Did Henry have any health problems that you were aware of—history of heart attack, diabetes, asthma?"

"Not that I know of," Mom said.

"How did Henry get along with Sonny?" Ted asked.

She shrugged. "Fine, as far as I know. This movie was the first time I'd ever worked with Sonny, but many of the other cast and crew members seemed to know him well. And they seemed to get along all right."

"What about Babs?" I finally felt I had something to contribute to the questioning. "Ron Fitz-patrick told me that Babs flirted with all the guys. Is it possible there was more to their relationship than mere flirting?"

Mom frowned. "Babs . . . and *Sonny*? I can't imagine those two being a couple . . . but I suppose anything is possible."

I made a mental note to ask Ron his opinion of Sonny's relationship with Babs. I had a few questions for Sonny too . . . although I knew they'd have to wait. If Henry hadn't died of natural causes, then next to Mom, Sonny would be the Tallulah County Police Department's main suspect in his death. I was sure the TCPD would be interrogating Sonny for hours about what he saw, how Henry had acted, whether or not he and Henry had argued, and if he'd noticed anything unusual this morning when he visited Henry.

By the time the pizza arrived, I was ready to put the events of the day behind us—to the extent possible—and veg out with a good movie.

"Let's take the pizza and some plates into the living room, sit on the floor and eat, and then watch a funny movie," I said.

"That sounds nice, dear, but I'm not really up to it," Mom said. "I'm not even hungry, so I'm going to go on upstairs."

I sighed as she left the kitchen. "I hate seeing her like this."

"I know, babe. So do I."

"What do you think about Henry's death?" I asked.

He ran a hand through his hair. "I hope the man died of natural causes. Maybe the stress was simply too much for him to bear, and he had a heart attack."

"Yeah, that's the best-case scenario. Give me the worst."

"Worst-case scenario is that Henry was murdered," Ted said. "Then the TCPD will try to tie Henry's murder to the murder of Babushka Tru."

"And they'll try to pin both on my mother," I said.

He pulled me close and kissed the top of my head. "Let's not get ahead of ourselves."

On Saturday morning, I left Angus home with Mom. She might not necessarily want actual human company, but I knew his companionship would do her good.

All the way to the Seven-Year Stitch, I thought about the events leading up to Henry's death. He was—or, at least, appeared to be—perfectly fine when I met with him yesterday morning. I mean, yes, he was distraught over Babs' death, but he didn't seem to be in any physical distress.

I sat down in the sit-and-stitch square to begin my new cross-stitch project. Sometimes getting started was the hardest part. My mind wandered back to the surveillance tape. As I separated threads, I thought about Sonny. If Henry had, in fact, died of unnatural causes, what reason would Sonny have to do him in? Had Henry seen something the morning of Babs' murder? Did Sonny *think* Henry had seen something? But if Henry had seen a viable suspect, wouldn't he have said as much to the police?

I placed my cloth into an embroidery frame and came to the conclusion that maybe Henry *had* said as much to the police. Maybe someone leaked something to Sonny or to the press, and that's why Sonny went to talk with Henry. I remembered seeing a uniformed Tallulah County Police Department deputy going into Henry's hotel room a few minutes before Sonny. It was a long shot, but Deputy Preston had been friendly to me. Maybe he could give me some sort of clue as to what had happened yesterday morning.

I set my framed cloth on the ottoman and went to my office to get Deputy Preston's card. I called his cell phone number and announced my identity when he answered. I realized, belatedly, that he'd probably seen my name come up on his caller ID.

"Oh, hey, Marcy," Deputy Preston said. "Is everything going okay?"

"Well. . . . I did wonder if you have a few minutes to chat. Is this a bad time?"

"No, it's not a bad time at all. In fact, I'm off today, and I'm down the street at MacKenzies' Mochas. Want me to stop by your shop?"

"Do you mind?" I asked.

"Not a bit," he said. "Want a coffee?"

"No, thank you, I'm good. But I appreciate your asking."

"Be there in a few."

After ending the call, I went back to the sit-and-stitch square. I threaded two needles—one with white floss and one with a pale blue—so I could concentrate on the tiny area in the center of the Monet print pattern. I'd work my way from the center out. I wished all of life's puzzles could be worked out that easily.

The bells over the door jingled, and I looked up expectantly. Instead of Deputy Preston, however, my visitors were customers. They were sisters who came in often on Saturdays to see if I had anything new.

"Anything good come in this week?" Janey asked. Janey was the shorter, skinnier of the two middle-aged women, but they both had the same sense of style. Both had chestnut-colored hair with auburn highlights, and they always wore bright red lipstick.

"Check this out," I said, leading them over to the Monet prints. "Aren't they gorgeous? I'm working on one now."

"They are beautiful," said Judy. "But I think they're a little too complicated for me. You got anything easier?"

"Judy, you're always selling yourself short," Janey said. "You could do this."

"I think she's right," I said. "The pattern is stamped on the fabric, so it shouldn't be as hard as it looks."

Judy scrunched up her face. "I don't know. I'm still afraid to try it." She looked at her sister. "You do it."

Janey put her fisted hands on her hips. "I'm not going to if you don't."

"If you want to move away from cross-stitch, I got some adorable needlepoint designs in this week," I said. I went over to the side of the board where the needlepoint kits were hanging. "Check out these angels that represent each season."

"Oh, those are pretty," Judy said. "What do you think, J? I could do summer, and you could do fall?"

Janey's eyes widened, as did her smile. "Yes! And we could enter them in the fair—maybe as a joint entry!"

The women looked at me and said simultaneously, "We'll take these two!"

We laughed as Deputy Preston came into the shop.

"This must be the place to be this morning," he

said, encompassing all three of us in his smile. "Things are dull as dishwater at the coffeehouse. Then I come in here, and it's all sunshine and laughter."

"Judy and Janey are always full of fun," I said.

Deputy Preston looked different out of uniform. You know how you get used to seeing a person present himself or herself a particular way, and then they look odd when "normally" dressed? He wore jeans, motorcycle boots, and a long-sleeved navy blue Henley shirt. He wore some type of medallion around his neck, but it was partially obscured by the collar of his shirt.

"I'll be right with you," I told him as I calculated the sisters' purchases and put them in separate Seven-Year Stitch bags. "Please bring them in when you've completed them. I'd love to see the finished products."

"We will," Janey promised. "If nothing else, we'll come by here on our way to enter them in the fair."

"Good luck!" I called as they left.

Deputy Preston gave me a comical grimace.

"What's that about?" I asked.

"They're both going to enter their projects in the fair?" he asked. "I hope one doesn't beat out the other. It could cause a family feud."

I smiled. "They said something about entering them as a joint project."

"You can do that?" he asked.

I shrugged. "For their sake, I hope so. I'm not all that familiar with fair rules and regulations."

"Neither am I. I did a little woodworking in my Boy Scout days, but then my uncle got me into riding motorcycles," he said. "Mom wasn't too happy with him for that."

"No, and I don't blame her," I said. "Motorcycles are fun—I've ridden them with friends—but they can be dangerous."

"They're not that bad. It's the cars on the road that don't have any respect for you that you have to watch out for."

"That's true. How old were you when you started riding?"

"I was ten," he said. "Uncle Joe got me a dirt bike. I never looked back."

"Did you do motocross?" I asked.

He nodded. "Yep. Won quite a few races."

"Why didn't you continue with it—professionally, I mean?"

"I wasn't good enough to make any real money at it," he said. "I still ride for fun. But you didn't want me to come by to talk about motorcycles. What's on your mind?"

"Henry Beaumont."

He wagged a finger. "Now you know I can't discuss an ongoing investigation with a civilian."

"I know," I said. "It's just that yesterday at the

police station, Mom, Ted, and I were watching the surveillance tape, and we saw a deputy go up to Henry's room at about eleven o'clock."

"Yep. That was me. I had some follow-up questions for Mr. Beaumont."

"Did he seem all right to you then?" I asked. "Did he look pale? Seem to be having any discomfort? Anything?"

Deputy Preston shook his head. "Appeared to be right as rain."

"Do you think he was murdered?" I asked.

"The cause of Mr. Beaumont's death has not yet been determined." He grinned to offset the official statement. "Look, the TCPD is looking at every angle. Trust us to get to the bottom of this, whether Mr. Beaumont was murdered or not."

"Do you think he was?"

"Marcy. . . ."

"I know, I know," I said quickly. "I'm sorry. It's just that my mom found him, and she was one of the last people to see Babs alive, and I'm worried for her."

"I understand," he said. "But, again, you need to trust us."

"It's hard to trust when your mother's life is at stake."

"I understand," he said softly. "We're doing everything we can."

"Thanks." I bit my lower lip. "Could you make

sure Detectives Ray and Bailey are talking with Sonny Carlisle? He was visiting Henry immediately before my mother."

"I'll do my best." He turned to leave. "Take care of yourself."

"Thanks."

I had made an imperceptible dent in my cross-stitch project when Vera swept through the door.

"I'm glad to see you're here today," she said. "I was afraid you might be sick or something. I came by yesterday but you'd left. I intended to call you last night but then one thing led to another, and I simply let time get away from me. I'm sorry for blathering on. Is everything okay?"

I blew out a breath. "I suppose you heard about Henry."

"Henry Beaumont? No. What about him?"

"He was found dead in his hotel room yesterday," I said.

"Oh, my goodness, how terrible! What happened?"

"The Tallulah County Police Department is currently looking into that. I had to leave yesterday because Mom was the one who found Henry."

"No! That poor dear," she said, coming over to the sofa to give me a quick hug. "And poor you.

This entire movie deal was supposed to be a dream job for you, and it has turned into a horrible nightmare."

"I don't know that I'd have called it a dream job," I said. "But it would have been nice to have worked with Mom."

"Well, maybe you'll get to work with her on another project. Surely they'll drop this one now that both the star *and* the producer-director are dead, won't they?" She gasped. "Wait. Do the police think the deaths are connected? What if both Babs and Henry were murdered to keep this movie from going forward? What if there's some deep dark secret about Sonam Zakaria that someone doesn't want revealed?"

I offered a tight smile. "Yeah . . . that would be something."

"Seriously, we just don't know, do we? I only hope that the killer doesn't think any of the rest of us know the secret and come after *us*." Her wide eyes took in the shop, as if the killer was going to jump up from behind one of the sofas wearing a mask and wielding a chain saw any second.

"Maybe Henry had a heart attack," I said. "We don't know there was anything nefarious at all about his death."

No sooner had those words left my mouth than Ted came rushing into the shop. "Marcy, you need to go home."

I leapt up off the sofa. "Is it Mom? What's happened?"

"The medical examiner smelled a bitter almond odor on Henry," he said. "He tested for cyanide and found that Henry was poisoned."

I frowned, not understanding why that would necessitate my going home.

"Detectives Bailey and Ray are getting a search warrant for your house," Ted continued. "Someone in the department alerted Manu. You should go home and be there when they arrive."

I turned toward Vera.

"Go," she said. "I'll watch the shop until you get back."

Chapter Twenty

Ted and I hurried to my house, where Mom, Alfred Benton, and Cam Whitting were already waiting.

"Manu told us what was going on," Ted said. "What can we do to help?"

"I think perhaps Angus would be more comfortable in another location," Alfred said.

"You're right. I hadn't thought of that, but we definitely don't want him here with crime scene techs tearing the house and yard apart," I said. I avoided looking at Mom. I hadn't meant that the way it sounded, but she took it that way anyway.

"I'm so sorry I've caused you so much trouble, Marcella. If I'd had any idea my coming here would've brought this mess down upon you, I'd never have come."

I sighed. "Mom, this isn't your fault."

She simply turned away and went into the kitchen.

I heaved another sigh. "I'm sorry. I didn't intend to sound like I blamed Mom in any way."

I looked at the three men. The two attorneys looked down at the floor, and Ted gave me a one-armed hug.

"It's all right, babe," Ted said. "Tensions are running high today. Why don't you take Angus over to the Stitch so Vera can keep an eye on him?"

I nodded. "That's a good idea. I'll be back as quickly as I can."

I retrieved Angus's leash from the entryway and called him to me. He bounded to me, excited that he was going to be taking a ride. He knew that most often when we were at home, I let him out into the backyard to play. Here, the leash meant he was going for a ride. At the shop, the leash meant he was going for a walk. Either way, Angus identified his leash with good things.

I'd followed Ted to my house in the Jeep, so I had Angus climb into the backseat and off we went. We met a car driven by Detective Bailey—Ray was in the passenger seat—on its way to my house. I sped up to five miles over the speed limit. I didn't want to risk getting a citation, but I wanted to hurry to the Seven-Year Stitch and get back before the crime scene techs started taking my house apart. Hopefully, Ted and the attorneys would make them be as neat and orderly as possible.

This entire situation made me angry. As if Mom would poison Henry Beaumont! It was ridiculous. Surely the police would see that . . . wouldn't they?

I pulled into one of the parking spaces in front of the Seven-Year Stitch. There was a customer there looking at embroidery floss.

"Ah, there she is!" the young woman said when Angus and I walked into the shop.

She was a regular customer, but her name escaped me at the moment. All I could think about was getting back home to Mom. Still, I realized the need to be polite. My problems were certainly not *her* fault. As if reading my mind, Angus sauntered over and nudged the customer in the rib cage with his big nose. She immediately began petting him and telling him what a sweet boy he was.

I saw Paul Samms sitting on the sofa beside Vera. I figured she'd called him as soon as Ted and I had left. He raised his hand in a friendly wave, and I waved back.

"Are you looking for anything in particular today?" I asked the customer, whose name I remembered was Trisha.

"I am," she said. "I need a soft pink metallic floss, but it appears you're all out."

"Let me check the storeroom." I went into the

storeroom, and sure enough, I had a few skeins of pink metallic floss. I brought them out. "Would this do?"

"That'll be perfect!"

I rang up her purchase, and she breezed out the door.

I stepped over to Vera and Paul. "I'm sorry to do this to you, but could you guys watch the shop just a little longer . . . and keep Angus with you? The attorneys didn't think it was such a good idea for Angus to be there during the search, but I want to go back while the crime scene techs are there."

"Of course you do," Vera said. "We'll stay as long as you need us to."

"And if you need us to lock up the shop and bring Angus home at closing time, we'll be happy to do that too," Paul added.

"I appreciate that, but I'll be sure to be back here before then," I said. I'd make a point of it. I didn't know Paul all that well, and I didn't want Mom to feel like I'd brought a reporter to see her being humiliated by the police while we were trying so desperately to keep the rest of the media in the dark. I thanked them again, and quickly left the shop before another customer arrived.

By the time I got back to my house, the crime scene technologists' truck was there. When I went inside, there were people I'd never seen before tramping around in my living room wearing latex gloves and paper booties. I was glad to see that they were at least not tracking dirt all over my carpet.

I went into the kitchen, where Detectives Bailey and Ray were heading up the search. They, too, had on gloves and booties. With their backs to me and unaware of my presence, I heard them talking about the case.

". . . rare to have a poisoning like this around here," Detective Ray was saying. "We've only had one other cyanide poisoning in the past five years."

"Yeah, but our suspects aren't *from around here*," Detective Bailey said. He looked over his shoulder and saw me standing there. "You're not allowed in this room while we're conducting our search, Ms. Singer."

"Where am I allowed to be?" I asked. "I'm looking for my mom and her *attorneys*." I stressed the word *attorneys* to remind them that they'd better be doing everything aboveboard. And although I knew better than to say it, there had better be another team of investigators searching Sonny Carlisle's hotel room.

"They're in the backyard," Detective Ray said.

"Thank you." I moved past them and went out onto the back porch. Mom and Alfred were sitting on the swing so often favored by Angus, while Ted and Cam were sitting in chairs. I sat on the picnic table and glared at the door. "Does anyone know yet whether or not Sonny Carlisle has been subjected to a search? After all, he was the one who was there before Mom arrived and found Henry unconscious."

"He has," Alfred said. "In fact, they searched his hotel room early this morning."

"Did they find anything?" I asked.

"They weren't at liberty to say," Alfred said. He and Ted shared a look. I caught the meaning. Had they found cyanide in Sonny's hotel room, they wouldn't be looking for it here.

"I'm sorry for all of this," Mom said. "I really am."

"Don't worry about it," I said. "It isn't the first time my home has been searched." It was then that I noticed a stern-looking uniformed deputy standing at the corner of the porch. I gave him a tight smile. He didn't smile back. He made me wish Deputy Preston hadn't been off duty today.

We sat there in silence for a long while, listening to the birds chirp, watching the grass grow, hoping the detectives wouldn't find anything linking my mother to Henry Beaumont's murder. I didn't *think* I had anything containing cyanide, but who knew? Could the drain cleaner contain cyanide? I played the phony commercial in my mind. *Smiling woman with beautifully coiffed hair and a double strand of pearls to complement her 1950s-style dress says, "With just a hint of cyanide, Drain Buster eats through anything that could clog your sink!" Voice-over man rapidly warns, "Keep Drain Buster out of reach of children, pets, elderly people, the mail carrier, rodents, and movie producers. May be harmful if swallowed, touched, inhaled, or looked at without protective eyewear."*

I glanced over at Mom. Alfred had placed a comforting hand over hers and was gently moving the swing back and forth. Mom looked pale and gaunt. She looked like she'd aged at least five years this week. She'd arrived in Tallulah Falls looking vibrant and healthy. She'd been lively and excited about the new movie. Now she looked tired and sad. And she wanted to go home to San Francisco. I could see it in her eyes. She wanted to go home and hide until this ugly situation had been resolved.

Finally, Ted cleared his throat. When I looked up at him, he told me it was nearly five o'clock.

I slapped my hand to my forehead. "Vera and Paul . . . and Angus." I turned to Mom. "We need to go get Angus and close up the shop. We'll still keep Angus away from here until the investigators are finished."

"It shouldn't be much longer now," Cam said. "This family has been inconvenienced long enough—actually, too long. Come back whenever you're ready. If the investigators don't like it, they can lump it. This is your home, and Angus is your dog. You aren't even under suspicion for anything."

"Thanks," I said. "We'll be back soon. Call my cell if you need us."

Ted and I went through the house to the Jeep.

I handed him my keys. "Do you mind driving? I don't feel up to it."

"I don't mind at all. In fact, it gives me something to do. I've been sitting and feeling helpless for so long, I could hardly wait to get out of there."

"Me too." I got into the Jeep and leaned back against the passenger seat. "When do you think this will all go away?"

"Soon," he said. "The detectives aren't going to find any cyanide in your house, are they?"

"I don't think so. It's not a common ingredient in any household cleansers or anything, is it?"

"No." He squeezed my hand. "They won't find anything, your mom will be let off the hook, and before long everything will be fine."

"Do you really believe that?" I asked.

He pursed his lips. "It won't happen that quickly, but I think it will happen."

"I should offer to buy Vera and Paul dinner for watching Angus and the shop," I said. "What do you think?"

"I think that's a good idea," he said. "Plus, if we get takeout and eat in the park, we can keep Angus away from home for a while longer and give the investigators time to finish up. Despite what Cam said, I don't want to antagonize the Tallulah County Police Department. They're already looking at your mom pretty hard for the murder of Babushka Tru. Now, they've added Henry's murder to the mix, so we don't need to give them any other reasons to be suspicious."

Vera and Paul were receptive to the idea of getting takeout and eating in the park. It was a warm, partly cloudy afternoon, so the weather was great for a picnic, even if my mood wasn't.

"And hopefully, these media hounds won't know about the park and won't find us there," Vera said. "No offense, darling"—this to Paul—"but once news of Henry Beaumont's poisoning is made public, those people are going to be swarming like flies."

"That's true," he said. "There's journalism and then there's . . . whatever it is they do. I'm not offended, V, because I don't consider myself one of those 'media hounds' as you call them."

"Good," she said, "because you certainly are not one of them. Well, boys, why don't you go get the food while we lock up here and take Angus on to the park?"

"That sounds good," Ted said. "Where should we meet?"

"We'll be near the dog park," I said. "I know

Angus will enjoy a good run. Get him something small that won't ruin his dinner, okay?"

That got a hearty laugh from all three of them, and I had to join in. There wasn't much that could spoil Angus's dinner. Supplement, yes. Spoil, no.

On the drive to the park, Vera asked me about Mom.

"How's Beverly holding up?"

"Not well," I said. "I was noticing today how drained she looks. This ordeal has taken a terrible toll on her."

"I can imagine," Vera said. "Do you think she'll continue to design costumes after this?"

The question blindsided me. "Of course I do. Why wouldn't she?"

Vera shrugged. "I didn't mean anything hateful by it, dear. I only meant that this might cause her so much distress that she won't want to do it again . . . that maybe she'd want to do something else . . . start a clothing line or something."

"Huh . . . I've never considered Mom not designing costumes," I said. "It's what she does . . . it's who she is." I made a mental note to talk with Mom about what, if any, life changes this movie experience might have evoked. I had been thinking about her beating murder charges. I hadn't thought about how the murders themselves had affected her and her career outlook.

We got to the park and turned Angus loose in the dog park. He immediately made friends with a boxer, and the two romped and played.

When the men returned, they had a bucket of fried chicken and a plan. According to Paul, we were going to "put our heads together" and figure out who'd want to kill both Henry Beaumont and Babushka Tru.

"It can't be a coincidence," Paul said. "The victims knew each other and worked together. Now, what all did they have in common?"

I'd brought Angus to the picnic table where Vera was using napkins to make a tablecloth. I looped the leash around the table leg and opened a small packet of wipes I keep in my purse.

"Well, the main thing is the movie," I said. "Maybe someone didn't want the movie to be made. I mean, Babs was killed, but Henry had held a press conference saying he was still planning to move forward." I cleaned my hands and threw the wipe into the trash can.

"Okay, the movie." Paul wrote The Movie at the top of a sheet of yellow legal paper. "What all do we know about the movie?"

"It was about an Indian film star named Sonam Zakaria," I said. "I'd never heard of her—and in fact thought it was a man—before Mom explained that she'd been a big deal in Bollywood. Manu and Reggie had heard of her. They thought she was great too, but I don't know that many other Americans would have been familiar with her . . . at least not until the film came out."

Paul was nodding. "Okay . . . okay. . . . What if someone didn't want the American public to become familiar with Sonam Zakaria?"

"I guess that's possible," I said. "But wouldn't they just do like other famous people and simply denounce the movie as a pack of lies?"

"Let's move on from Sonam Zakaria," Ted said. "Is there any other reason that someone would want to keep this movie from being made?"

I gave him a grateful smile. I knew him well enough to realize that he was merely placating Paul. Ted didn't think the movie was the link Henry and Babs shared that got them both killed, and I agreed with him.

"I can't think of a single reason anyone wouldn't want the movie made," Vera said. "It was BTru's big chance at a comeback; there was already some Oscar buzz about it. . . . In fact, I think it'll still get made. It'll just be delayed until they find a new producer and star."

"Vera's right," I said. "Too much has been invested in this movie for it to be abandoned altogether. Let's look at other angles . . . like the fact that Henry had just learned prior to casting Babushka in the role that he was her biological father."

Vera's and Paul's almost-identical reactions were comical. Their lower jaws nearly bounced off the picnic table.

I laughed. "Close your mouths, guys, before a mother bird comes and feeds one of you a worm."

Vera was the first to sputter back to life. "Is that true? Says who? When did you find that out? Were you holding out on me?"

"I didn't find it out until yesterday morning when Henry told me," I said. "I went to his hotel room because Mom was so upset because she thought he was having an affair with Babs. He said he wasn't having an affair with her and that she was his biological daughter. Mita Trublonski had told him a few months ago."

"Well, this changes everything," Paul said. "How did Babs feel about Henry being her father?"

"She didn't know," I said. "Henry said that he and Mita had decided to keep it from Babs at least until the movie was finished. They didn't want her to think Henry had given her the part because she was his daughter."

"How did Henry's wife feel about his having a daughter?" Vera asked.

"He said she'd been hurt at first, but that she quickly adapted to the news," I said. "They'd been unable to have children of their own. Henry seemed to cling to Babs as if she were some sort of miracle, and I believe he hoped Eileen would come to feel the same way."

Vera snorted. "Fat chance."

"Speaking of Eileen, she was supposed to be coming in today," I said. "Surely, after the police called her with the news of Henry's death yesterday, she decided not to come."

"Or she might be coming to take his body back home," Ted said.

"I should check and see," I said. "Maybe she didn't get over those hurt feelings as easily as Henry had thought. She could've slipped something into his shaving kit that he hadn't used until this morning. That's possible, isn't it?"

"Anything's possible," Ted said.

Chapter Twenty-one

Once everyone had left to give Mom and me some time alone on Saturday evening, I put on soft classical music and made us mugs of hot chocolate with whipped cream and chocolate sprinkles. Mom added a splash of Irish crème to hers. Then we sank onto the sofa in the living room.

"So, how are you?" I asked. Before she could answer something flippant, I added, "I know it's rather like asking Mary Todd Lincoln, 'Other than that, how was the play?' but, seriously, how are you feeling?"

"I'm feeling overwhelmed," she answered. "And scared . . . no, make that terrified . . . and sad. Henry had been a close friend for so long. . . . You know, when I first stepped into that room, I never dreamed he'd been murdered. I was thinking heart attack, aneurysm . . . anything but murder."

"And yet you knew not to touch anything even before Ted warned you not to, didn't you?"

"I haven't been in the movie business for as long as I have without picking up something from police procedurals." She sipped her chocolate. "Everyone liked Henry. He was good to cast and crew members. He was thoughtful. I can't imagine anyone wanting him dead. Babushka, yes. I understand why someone would want to push her off a ledge or bash her head in. But Henry? No."

"Mom! I'm surprised at you. That's a horrible thing to say about Babs."

"You asked me how I'm feeling," she said. "I thought you wanted me to be honest."

"I do," I said. "I'm sorry. I know Babs treated everyone horribly. But if Henry really was her father, then there must've been something good about her . . . even if it was buried way below the surface . . . right?"

"I guess." She sighed. "I feel so sorry for Eileen."

"Do you think she'll come to Tallulah Falls, or do you expect her to have Henry's body sent home with a police escort?" I asked.

"Knowing Eileen, she'll be here, if she isn't already. She'll want to talk with the police and determine exactly what happened to Henry. And she won't go back home until they release the body to her." She studied her mug for a second. "I'll call her cell tomorrow. If she's in town, maybe I can offer her a meal . . . a shoulder to cry on . . . my condolences."

I patted Mom's arm. "Just keep in mind I'm here for you in case you need a shoulder."

She smiled. "Thanks."

"What do you think you'll do when you get home?" I asked. "Will you want to take some time off before taking on a new project, or do you want to dive right back in?"

"I don't know," she said. "Whether I'm arrested or not, if a cloud of suspicion is hanging over my head, I doubt anyone will want to hire me."

"You know that's not going to happen," I said. "You did nothing wrong, and you're going to be exonerated."

"Yeah . . . I hope so."

"Vera is afraid this nightmare will put you off costuming forever," I said lightly. "She thinks that if it does, you should start your own clothing line."

"Does she now?" She took a drink of her chocolate and licked the whipped cream from the corner of her mouth. "Creating my own clothing line, huh? That does sound intriguing."

The next morning, I got up early and made a double batch of oatmeal raisin muffins. I packed up half the muffins and put the rest under a lidded cake plate. I kissed Angus's nose and left Mom a note telling her I had to run an errand and would be back as soon as possible.

I was on my way to the hotel to see Sonny Carlisle to determine what I could learn about his visit to Henry yesterday morning. I felt he was a more viable suspect than anyone else who'd been in Henry's hotel room, but I wasn't sure he'd killed Henry either. I had my cover story worked out, and I called Sonny from the lobby to ask if he could see me. I said I had muffins but that if it was too early for a social call, I'd leave them for him at the front desk. He told me to bring them up.

Sonny was dressed and looked as if he'd been up for a while when he opened the door. He had on a tracksuit, and I guessed he'd been in the fitness room.

"Have you had breakfast yet?" I asked.

"Just a glass of OJ on the way to walk on the treadmill for two miles," he said. "Those smell awfully good. What kind are they?"

"Oatmeal raisin."

"I love oatmeal raisin! Come on in and have a seat," he said.

I knew he liked oatmeal raisin cookies because I'd seen him taking some from the food cart once when I visited Mom on set. I was hoping that meant he liked oatmeal raisin muffins too.

We sat down at the table. Sonny had opened the curtains, and we had an excellent view of the town.

"Want some coffee?" he asked. "I made some in this little pot this morning, but it's probably too cold and strong to drink. But I can have room service bring up a pot."

"I'm fine, but if you want some, please go ahead."

He grinned. "I definitely want some." He called room service and requested a coffee tray. Then he sat back down across from me. "So, what brings you by, Marcy?"

"I figure you and Mom are pretty much in the same boat," I said. "I know she's upset right now and in need of comfort food. I guessed you might be too."

"I am," he said. "Henry was a good friend."

"Well, not only that, but now the movie is kaput, right?" I asked.

"I suppose it is. I hadn't stopped to give it much thought, but I don't know who'd take it on after all this."

I plunged on ahead. "Sonny, I know you were one of the last people to see Henry alive." At the sharp rise of his brows, I added, "The Tallulah County Police Department had us watch the surveillance tape to see if we could identify anyone, and we saw you arrive just a few minutes before Mom did."

There came a knock at the door. "Let me get

that," he said. He got up and held open the door while the room service waiter rolled the cart in with the coffee tray. He then tipped the waiter and shut the door.

He poured two cups of coffee and set them on the table. He put the baskets containing sweetener and creamer on the table too, and then he sat down. He didn't look back up at me until he'd put sugar and creamer into his coffee.

"Are you accusing me of something, Marcy?" he asked.

"Not at all," I said. "I'm just thinking that if we put our heads together on this, maybe we can figure out what happened."

His face was still hard and untrusting.

"Henry told me yesterday morning that Babushka Tru was his daughter," I said.

That got Sonny's attention. His eyes widened, and once again, his eyebrows shot up. "Are you serious?"

"Completely. I saw him before I went into work yesterday," I said. "He was so upset over Babs' death. Mom had been angry with him because she misconstrued his affection for Babs—she thought they were having an affair—and I came to talk with him. That's when he told me she was his daughter. He said Mita Trublonski told him a few months ago, but they hadn't told Babs yet."

"Why wouldn't they tell her?" he asked.

"Henry said that he and Mita didn't want Babs to think her comeback was all because of their relationship."

"But it was." Sonny took a muffin and tore it in half. "I can't imagine keeping a secret like that. Did Eileen know?"

I nodded. "Henry said she was upset at first but came to accept it. Once the police determined that Henry had been poisoned, I wondered if she really had accepted it."

He'd bitten into the muffin but couldn't resist speaking with his mouth full. "What? You think Eileen poisoned Henry?"

"She had both the motive and the opportunity," I said. "She could've put the cyanide into his shampoo or mouthwash or something before he even left for Oregon."

Sonny swallowed while shaking his head. "Nah, I don't think so. He'd have died a lot sooner then, wouldn't he? I mean, we all use that stuff every day."

"Maybe she put it in a new bottle, and he finished up his old bottle first," I said.

Again, Sonny shook his head. "No. Not Eileen. Besides, if the police had found the cyanide in Henry's stuff here, why would they have kept looking?"

"To see if you or Mom had something similar," I said.

"They went through your stuff too?" he asked.

"Yep. Mom is the one who found Henry's body," I said. "Didn't they tell you that?"

"They didn't tell me much of anything." He took another bite of muffin. "I still say it wasn't Eileen, though. I've known her for a long time. A killer, she ain't."

"Then it just about had to be someone here," I said. "How did Henry seem when you saw him?"

"He was jittery . . . sweating, breathing hard. . . . He kept putting his hands up to his temples." Sonny took a drink of his coffee. "I didn't want to leave him like that, so I asked him to let me call an ambulance for him."

"What did he say?"

"He said no—said he probably just had a little touch of food poisoning from his breakfast," he said.

"Maybe that's it," I said. "Maybe somebody bribed one of the hotel workers to put the poison in Henry's food."

"I'm sure the police are taking all that into consideration. Don't get so worked up."

"How can I not get worked up, Sonny? My mother is under suspicion for Henry's death . . . and so are you. How can *you* not get worked up?"

"I know I'm innocent," he said. "And I believe in our justice system. Let the police do their jobs. That's what I'm doing."

"Okay," I said. I looked at my watch, even though I had nowhere I had to be at any particular time. "I really should be going."

"Well, now, you just trust that everything will be all right," Sonny said. "And thank you for the muffins. They're delicious."

"You're welcome." I turned back toward him when I got to the door. "If you think of anything, will you let me know?"

"Sure," he said.

Somehow, I wasn't very confident about that.

As I was waiting for the elevator, Ron Fitzpatrick came down the hall.

"Hey, Marcy," he said. "What're you doing here?"

"I stopped by to see Sonny for a minute. He seems pretty upset over Henry's death," I said.

"Yeah, we all are."

The elevator doors opened, and Ron and I walked inside.

"I'm going to breakfast," he said, as the doors closed. "Want to join me?"

"No, thanks. I need to get home and check on Mom. This past week has really taken a toll on her," I said.

"I heard that." He shook his head. "First Babs

and then Henry? It's like somebody's gone nuts . . . like the whole *world* has gone nuts!"

"I know. Hey, you mentioned you had promo and outtake footage that you submitted to news and entertainment outlets," I said. "I'd love to see it."

"And I'd be happy to show it to you, but I really am starving."

"Can we do it later today?" I asked. "You could come to my house, we could have snacks. . . . Angus would try to cajole you into a game of fetch. . . ."

"Yeah, sounds good," he said. "Just tell me when and where."

I gave him my address, and he agreed to come by at around one o'clock that afternoon.

When I got out to the Jeep, I called Ted and asked if he could make it.

"I'll be there," he said. "But are you sure a movie clip party is really what your mom needs right now?"

"I think it might be exactly what we all need. Maybe we'll see something that will help us find the person who killed both Babs and Henry."

He chuckled. "All right, Inch-High. I'll see you at one."

Okay, I'll admit it was a stretch. No one was going to walk by wearing a sandwich sign reading I hate Babs on one side and I hate Henry on the other. But we might see something that would give us a clue.

I pulled onto my street and noticed a strange car parked in my driveway. It was a black sedan, and my fear that it was a police officer or journalist hassling my mother made me whip into the driveway sideways, throw the Jeep into park, and rush into the house with guns-a-blazing. Not that I had any guns to blaze, but I'm talking attitude here. I had attitude—plenty of attitude.

"Mom! Are you all right?" I called as I opened the door, ready to do battle with the unknown, unwanted guest.

"I'm in the kitchen, darling. Come and meet Eileen," Mom said.

Eileen. Eileen Beaumont. So I'd overreacted. But, in my defense, Eileen still hadn't been ruled out as a killer yet . . . at least not in my book.

"I'll be right there!" I called. I went back outside, got in the Jeep—whose door I'd left open—and parked properly . . . and then I got out, closed the door, and went back into the house.

When I went into the kitchen, I saw that Mom was making crepes.

"Hi, sweetie," Mom said. "Are you hungry?"

"No, thanks," I said. I walked to the table and

extended my right hand toward Eileen. "Hi, I'm Marcy."

"We've met before actually," said Eileen, a woman with wavy caramel brown hair and dark eyes. "You were just a little girl then. I'm not surprised you don't remember me."

"Wait. It was at a cast party, wasn't it?" I asked, vaguely remembering Eileen Beaumont in a long peach gown smiling and nodding at everyone who spoke to her.

"It was," Eileen said.

"See?" Mom asked. "I told you she'd remember."

I pulled out a chair and sat down. "I'm sorry for your loss, Eileen. It must've come as quite a shock."

"Yes, it did," she said. "I keep turning the whole thing over and over in my mind. First Babs and then Henry. I can't imagine who'd want to hurt either of them . . . but *both*? It's almost unbelievable." Her eyes filled with tears. "And yet the person whose face I keep seeing in my mind is that of Mita Trublonski. I can't help but feel that somehow she's responsible for everything."

Chapter Twenty-two

Eileen Beaumont had left long before Ron Fitz-patrick had arrived, but what she'd said about Mita Trublonski lingered. I couldn't imagine Mita harming her own child, but if she thought Henry was responsible for Babs' death, she might strike out at him. I intended to look at the footage closely to see if Ms. Trublonski was in any of the footage and, if she was, how she'd behaved toward Henry.

Ted had called me back before coming over and asked if I'd mind another set of experienced eyes seeing the film footage. I'd said of course I didn't, so Manu and Reggie joined our viewing party. Ted and the Singhs arrived in separate vehicles but at roughly the same time. Ron arrived at one o'clock on the dot. I'd baked some mini-quiches I had in the freezer along with brownies and peanut butter cookies. Mom had made a cheese ball and placed it on a tray with an assortment of crackers. I felt as if we were in good shape refreshment-wise.

We arranged everything on a decorative platter and took it into the living room. It was a mild, sunny day, so I put Angus out into the backyard with a granola bone until after everyone had had their fill of the refreshments. Even with the platter placed on the highest surface of the living room, it wouldn't be safe from a dog of Angus's considerable height . . . and appetite.

"Hey," Ron said when he came in carrying his equipment bag. "I didn't know there'd be so many people here."

"Well, you know Reggie," I said. "This is her husband Manu, and this is Ted Nash." I decided not to reiterate the fact that we were looking for murder suspects, especially since Ron seemed a little nervous. "At the rate things are going, this might be our only chance to see any of the movie."

"Yeah," he said. "It might. Hope not, though. That'd be a shame. I saw Angus outside—told him I'd play with him before I leave."

"I thought I'd bring him back in after we have our snacks," I said.

He glanced over at the platter. "Oh, that's smart. Chocolate is bad for dogs."

"I know." I smiled. "Is there anything you need to get set up?"

"Nope. I'll just plug into your TV, if that's all right."

"That's fine," I told him.

Ted, Mom, and Reggie were sitting on the sofa. Manu was on the armchair. I was planning to sit on the ottoman, but that left Ron without a seat. I went into the kitchen to retrieve a chair. By the time I got back, Ron had set up a computer with the digital equipment on the ottoman and pulled it close enough to the television to hook in the required cables. I went back for another chair.

Instead of sitting on a chair, however, Ron sat on the floor in front of the ottoman so he could work the equipment to show us the film footage. I placed my chair beside Manu. He gave me a smile and a nod, as if to reassure me that we'd certainly see something in Ron's footage that would help us to discover the identity of Babs' and Henry's murderer or murderers. I doubted he was really all that confident. I wasn't, but like everything else as far as investigating this case went, it couldn't hurt.

The first clip that came up on my TV screen featured Babs in full Sonam Zakaria costume back in San Francisco. She was batting her lashes and flirting with someone offscreen. She even blew the person a kiss.

"Okay," Henry was saying. "Can we please get

the shot this time? We're getting behind schedule. Babs, sweetie, I know you'll nail it this time." His *I know* sounded more like an *I'm praying*.

Babs gave him a saucy shrug and then sauntered over to her mark.

Henry gave the command to "Roll 'em."

Babs said her line and apparently did well because Henry called "Cut" and Babs walked off the set, winking at the camera as she did so.

The next clip was from Oregon. Again, Babs was in a flirtatious frame of mind. This time she was flirting with both Sonny and Henry. Someone said in a singsong voice that Babs had a boyfriend, and she told the man in an angry tone to shut up. The camera panned around to the other people who were on the set. I recognized Ron, a makeup artist, and Deputy Preston.

"What's Deputy Preston doing there?" I asked.

"He was one of the patrolmen assigned to security detail," Ron said.

On-screen, Babs was shouting, "Where's my phone?" She followed up with the same question followed by a few choice expletives.

Ron laughed. The rest of us didn't.

"Did she ever find her phone?" Manu asked.

"Oh, sure. It was found in her dressing room later that day," Ron said. "It had probably been there all along."

"I didn't know her—I only met her once," Reggie said. "But Babs seemed to have been pretty bratty."

"She wasn't after you got to know her," Ron said. "Sure, she could be difficult—all great actresses can be—but she was so beautiful and so talented. . . . I think any man would've gone overboard to please her." He laughed. "You should've seen us all scrambling around trying to find her phone."

"Did Mita Trublonski visit the set often?" I asked.

"She didn't drop by all that much," Ron said. "When she did, though, I could tell that Babs and her mom didn't have the world's best relationship. I always got the impression that Mita was jealous of Babs . . . that she wanted Babs' fame and attention."

"What about Mita and Henry?" Ted asked. "Did they get along well?"

"They were civil." Ron pulled up the next clip. "Mostly, though, they avoided each other."

The rest of the footage contained scenes from the movie with a couple outtakes of actors—other than Babs—flubbing their lines.

"Didn't Babs ever make a mistake?" Reggie asked.

Ron grinned. "Not that she'd let us retain on film."

* * *

After Ron left, Angus lay at Reggie's feet and enjoyed having her scratch behind his ears.

"He certainly was infatuated with Babs, wasn't he?" Reggie asked.

"Yes, he was," Mom said. "And I, for one, disagree with his assessment that she got along well with all the men. A few of them might've been hoodwinked like Ron, but many of them saw through her petty, manipulative machinations."

"If I were investigating this for the Tallulah County Police Department, I'd first try to determine whether we were dealing with one killer or two," Manu said. "Detectives Bailey and Ray are adamant that Babs was killed by a blow to the head and they maintain that they have the murder weapon."

"And yet a couple people still insist that Babs' death might've been an accident," I said.

"Maybe that's what they want to believe . . . or want *you* to think they believe," Ted said.

"Here's what I'm thinking," Manu said. "What if Henry's killer thought Henry killed Babs?" He turned to Mom. "Beverly, didn't you say you saw Henry headed in Babs' direction after you left her that morning?"

"Yes, I did. But I never thought he killed her," Mom said. "I mean, the thought crossed my mind, but I dismissed it as being ridiculous. What made me angry toward Henry was the thought that he was the father of Babs' baby."

"And that's something else that could've made the killer angry," Ted pointed out. "No one seemed to know Babs was pregnant until after she was dead."

"So what we need to determine—I mean, what Detectives Ray and Bailey need to determine—is whether they're dealing with one killer or two and the motives behind the murders," Reggie said.

Ted had a white dry-erase board across an entire wall in his home office. I wish I had something similar to help us brainstorm. Since I didn't, I went into the kitchen and got a piece of paper. I made five columns: One Killer, Two Killers, Movie-Related Motive, Love Motive, and Other.

"Let's list everything we know or can guess into these columns," I said. "If it supports the one-killer theory, we'll put it in that column. That way, we can sort out our thoughts and see what we've got when we're finished."

"Okay," Manu said. "Put *unrequited love* into the two-killers column."

"What about Eileen Beaumont?" I asked. "Should we put her into a column?"

Manu frowned. "I don't know anything about her. Is she the wife of the deceased?" He shook his head as if to clear out the police jargon. "I mean, is she Henry's wife?"

"She is," Mom said. "She's in town trying to learn whatever she can from the police, and she came to brunch today. I believe she's innocent, but Marcella seems to think Eileen was upset enough over learning that Henry had an affair more than twenty years ago to slip some poison into his shampoo."

"He had an affair that produced a child," I said.

"Marcy has a point," Reggie said. "No matter how nice someone seems, that person could still turn out to be the killer. But since Eileen Beaumont was in San Francisco—wasn't she?—when Babs died, I think we should put her in the two-killers column too."

"What about Ron?" I asked. "Do you think it's possible he could've found out Babs was pregnant and been enraged enough at both her and Henry to kill them both?"

"Maybe, but it's doubtful," Ted said. "He wasn't on the surveillance tape visiting Henry's room that day."

"But he could've put the poison in something some time other than that morning," I said.

"All right then. Put him in the one-killer column," Ted said with a grin.

"I'm just trying to cover all the bases," I said.

"I know," he said. "And you're wonderful."

"Don't you guys start with the lovey-dovey stuff," Manu teased. "We're brainstorming here. What about Mita Trublonski? Does she raise any red flags with anyone?"

"She did with Eileen," Mom said. "Eileen seems to think everything is Mita's fault. She was bitterly adamant about that."

"Which goes back to my reasoning that she could be our killer," I said. "Even if she *was* in San Francisco, she could've got someone to hit Babs over the head and push her over the ledge."

"We've moved on from the subject of Eileen," Mom said. "Right now, we're talking about Mita Trublonski and the fact that she's just as probable a suspect as anyone."

"She might do Henry in," I said. "But I don't think she'd kill her own daughter."

"I can't imagine her killing either one," Reggie said. "She didn't really strike me as a woman of much substance. Why would she get rid of either of her meal tickets?"

"What about the movie angle?" Ted asked. "Could there be someone that was so desperate this movie not be made that they were willing to kill to stop it?"

"I don't know why they would," Manu said. "Sonam Zakaria isn't that big a name in the United States. I can't imagine any of her family or fellow countrymen sabotaging the movie because they dislike its content."

"Maybe they were spending too much money on it," Mom said. "Henry was pulling out all the stops for his little princess. I wouldn't be surprised to learn that the film was over budget despite the short time we'd been filming."

I looked over at Ted who had his chin resting on his steepled fingers. "What is it?" I asked him. "You're giving something some serious thought."

"I keep thinking back to the gunman we found dead there on Monday morning," he said. "Maybe instead of looking at the possibility of there being three isolated murders, we should consider the fact that they might all be related somehow."

Manu inclined his head. "I wonder if Detectives Bailey and Ray have looked at that."

"We should find out," Ted said.

Chapter Twenty-three

Monday morning, I was sitting in the sit-and-stitch square working on my impressionist cross-stitch project. Once again, Angus had stayed home with Mom. I missed him, but I realized she needed him right now. He'd hopefully be back at the Seven-Year Stitch where he belonged soon, and Mom would be out from under the dark cloud of suspicion and back at work.

The bells over the door jingled, and I looked up to see Sadie. She joined me in the sit-and-stitch square, peeping at my project before sitting down on the sofa.

"That looks majorly complicated," she said.

"It's not as bad as it looks. I think it'll be pretty when it's finished," I said. "I'm going to frame it and give it to Mom."

"She'll love that." Sadie glanced around the

shop. "Did Angus stay at home with her again today?"

I nodded. "It does her good to have him with her. He stays right by her side, and she spoils him rotten."

"So it's a win-win . . . at least for them," she said.

"Yeah. It gets lonely here for me. If it wasn't for the fact that the media is still hanging around, she could bring him here and hang out."

"Yeah . . . I guess the media swarm is even worse now that Henry Beaumont has died."

"At least they aren't camped out in front of my house," I said. "The police have done a good job of keeping the fact that Mom found his body out of the media. I don't think it's even been leaked to any blogs."

"That's good," Sadie said. "Has any progress been made on the investigation into Henry's death?"

"They learned on Saturday that he was poisoned." I gave Sadie a wary look. "They searched my house and yard. I brought Angus here, and Vera and Paul watched him and minded the shop."

"That's terrible!" She frowned. "Of course, they didn't find anything . . . did they?"

"No . . . and they searched Sonny Carlisle's hotel room too, so Mom wasn't the only suspect."

"Did they find anything on Sonny?" she asked.

"Not that I know of," I said. "The Tallulah County Police Department is keeping most of their information to themselves with regard to the murders of Babs and Henry. They're only sharing what they absolutely *have* to with Manu."

"How's your mom holding up?"

I shrugged. "As well as can be expected. Right now, she can't do much more than wait to see what happens next."

Sadie smiled. "I know that's not all *you're* doing."

I grinned too. "I'm doing everything I can to help the Tallulah County detectives find the real killer, despite the fact that they desperately don't want my help."

"I need to be getting back, but before I go, I want to ask you, Ted, and Beverly to dinner before class tomorrow evening," she said. "I'm taking tomorrow off, and Blake is going to leave at five o'clock. I'm making chicken cordon bleu, and I'd love to have you guys join us."

"That sounds great," I said. "I'll check with Ted and Mom and make sure that works for them. Thank you."

"You're welcome. I hope you can make it."

Sadie left as a customer came through the door.

*   *   *

I was helping a customer find a sturdy needlepoint yarn later that morning when Deputy Preston came into the shop. He was out of uniform, and today he wore jeans and a V-neck sweater. He gave me a polite wave and then wandered around the shop while he waited for the customer to make her purchase and leave.

"Hey, there," I said, approaching him as the customer walked out the door.

"Morning, Marcy," he said. "I'm off today, but I worked yesterday and saw the report on where they'd searched your house and all. I'm glad they didn't find anything incriminating on your mom, but I know she must be upset over everything. Is she doing okay?"

"She's fine," I said. "Thanks for asking. You . . . you don't know whether anyone else emerged as a more viable suspect after Saturday . . . do you?"

Deputy Preston laughed. "Now, Marcy, you know I'm not at liberty to tell you how the search went at Sonny Carlisle's hotel room . . . even if they didn't find anything there either."

"Thanks . . . I mean, for explaining why you can't tell me."

The sunlight glinted off the medallion he wore, and I examined it more closely. The letters TCMSA were embossed on the round pendant.

"What's wrong?" he asked.

"Nothing," I said. "I was just noticing your medallion. What do the letters stand for?"

"Tallulah County Mud Slingers Association," he said.

"Mud Slingers? Is that a political group?"

"No." He laughed. "We ride dirt bikes."

"Oh, I get it. That's cool," I said. "I think I've seen a medallion similar to this before. It was where the movie was being filmed. Is that a popular bike-riding trail?"

"Yeah, a lot of guys ride over there . . . experienced riders, that is . . . even though they're not supposed to. The terrain is challenging, but the view is beautiful. Or so they tell me."

"Did you know the guy who was found shot to death on the trail just before Henry Beaumont began filming there?" I asked.

"No."

"Hmm. I thought maybe he was a mud slinger," I said.

"Why would you think that? Was there a bike found near him?" he asked.

"No, but there was a dirt biker coming over the hill just before we stumbled upon the body," I said. "Of course, you probably read all that in the report."

"Yeah, I glanced at it," Deputy Preston said. "But, to be honest, I was more interested in the movie than I was in the body. I know that sounds bad, but I got caught up in all the Hollywood excitement."

"That's easy to do," I said. "By the way, you were caught on film when one of the cameramen was recording an outtake. You looked pretty impressive. Have you ever considered a movie career?"

He chuckled and lowered his head. "Me? No way. I don't think I have the talent for that. Besides, I'm taking criminal justice courses at Tallulah County Junior College. I just want to move up in the career I already have."

"Well, I'm sure you'll do that," I said.

Just then, one of my regular customers, a woman in her midsixties named Christine, came barreling through the door. Christine is normally a bundle of barely contained energy, and today the energy was less contained than usual.

"Marcy," she said breathlessly, thrusting a piece of felt in my direction. "Please help me with this blanket stitch. It's driving me bananas." She glanced at Deputy Preston. "Sorry for interrupting, but this is an emergency."

He grinned and waved good-bye. "See you later, Marcy."

"Enjoy your day off, Deputy Preston."

"Deputy?" Christine asked. "I figured he was just some hoodlum in here hitting on you."

I laughed. "Nevertheless, you have an emergency. Let's sit down here and work on that blanket stitch."

At lunchtime, Ted brought burgers, fries, and a new chew toy for Angus.

"I didn't know whether he'd be here or whether you'd leave him home with your mom, but we can always give it to him later," Ted said.

"You're so thoughtful."

"What can I say? You bring out my sensitive side." He winked.

I locked the front door and put the clock on the window stating that I'd be back in thirty minutes. Then Ted and I went into my office to eat.

"Before I forget, Sadie came over and invited the two of us and Mom to have dinner with her and Blake tomorrow before my class," I said. "She's making chicken cordon bleu. And trust me, Sadie makes fantastic chicken cordon bleu."

"Sounds good," he said, getting our food out of the bag while I retrieved sodas from the minifridge.

"It's been a little hectic today, so I haven't called Mom to ask her yet. Maybe I'll get a chance later this afternoon." I opened the box of fries. "Deputy Preston came by this morning. It's his day off, but he said he was concerned about Mom. In a roundabout way, he let me know that nothing was found in Sonny's hotel room either."

"Deputy Preston was concerned about your mom?" Ted asked. "Has he even met her?"

"I don't know," I said. "Maybe he met her on the movie set. He did strike me as being a little starstruck over the whole Hollywood thing."

"Yeah, wasn't he the one in the outtake yesterday?"

"He was. I asked him if he was interested in a movie career, but he said he wasn't." I poured a packet of ketchup on the empty side of my burger box. "He says he just wants to advance in his law enforcement career and is taking criminal justice classes at the community college."

"Well . . . good for him." Ted frowned as he took a drink of his soda. "I might have to watch that guy though. It sounds like he might have a crush on you."

"Nah. Like I said, I get the feeling he's starstruck. When the movie people ship out, he'll move along," I said. "Besides, my heart belongs to someone else."

He grinned.

We both dived into our food. After a couple minutes, Ted told me that while I'd had a hectic day, his had been fairly quiet.

"I even had time to do a little on-the-side investigating," he said. "Remember the outtake where Babs had lost her phone?"

I nodded.

"I managed to find out the name of Babs' accountant, and on a hunch, I called and asked him if any of her financial accounts had been hacked."

"Had they?" I asked.

"Yep. Two of her credit card accounts had been hacked and the bills ran up the day Babs died," Ted said. "The accountant said she was livid over it."

"And you think the fact that the credit card accounts were hacked had something to do with her losing her phone?"

He nodded. "It's the same MO as the gunman and his partner. That was one of their rackets— steal smartphones and hack financial accounts. They're bound to have felt like they hit the mother lode when Henry Beaumont brought his film crew to Tallulah Falls."

"But how is that possible?" I asked. "The gunman was dead by then. He died the day before the film crew arrived."

"True," said Ted. "But he had a partner. Just because the partner was tired of the gunman didn't mean he was tired of the money they were making off their criminal activities. My guess is that he found another hacker."

"And another victim—Babs," I said. "Maybe you were right yesterday when you said that it's possible all three murders are connected."

During the afternoon lull in business that often comes around three o'clock on weekdays, I called Mom and told her that Sadie had invited her, Ted, and me to dinner tomorrow evening before I head back to class.

"What do you think?" I asked. "Is that doable?"

"Yes, that works for me," she said.

"Are you all right? You sound tired. Did you sleep okay?"

"Hey, who's the mom here?" She chuckled softly. "I'm fine. I am a little tired . . . or maybe weary is the better word. I love being with you, Marcella, but not under these circumstances. I want all this to be over. I want to go home."

"I want that too, Mom." My eyes widened as I considered the possibility that she might misunderstand what I was saying. "I mean, I want the murder investigations to be over. I don't want you to go home." I didn't like the sound of that one either and decided to try once more. "What I'm saying is that, I want you to go home when you'd like to go home, but—"

"Relax," she interrupted. "I get what you're saying."

"Thanks. Hey, were you on the set that day when Babs lost her phone?"

"Yes. I thought it was mainly just another excuse to throw an elaborate tantrum," she said. "Babs was famous for those. Why?"

"Ted checked with Babs' accountant and learned that two of her credit card accounts were hacked on the day her smartphone went missing," I said. "He thinks now that all three murders—the gunman Reggie stumbled upon in the woods, Babs and Henry—could be connected somehow. If the gunman-slash-hacker had a partner who stole Babs' phone to hack the accounts, then he might've ultimately killed Babs and Henry."

"Wait," Mom said. "I'm not following you. If the gunman-slash-hacker was dead, then why would his partner steal Babs' phone? And furthermore, why would he kill her?"

"Ted thinks the partner has found another hacker. Maybe Babs caught the thief putting her phone back, and he killed her."

"I don't think so," Mom said. "Babs had her phone back before she died."

"Okay," I said. "But Ted said the accountant told him she was livid that her accounts had been hacked. Apparently, the thieves ran up some serious bills on her."

"Again, I think that was just Babs being dramatic," she said. "Sure, it's horrible that her accounts were hacked, but I'm certain that the companies wouldn't make her pay since she caught it in time. I mean, that's what they have fraud insurance for, right?"

"That's true. Maybe the three deaths aren't connected after all," I said. "But it would be kind of nice if they were . . . if they had nothing to do with the movie whatsoever . . . then you could be cleared to go home."

"Since two of the main players in this movie were killed, though, I doubt that's the case," Mom said.

"Yeah . . . I suppose you're right. But it *was* a nice thought."

Chapter Twenty-four

I was sitting in the sit-and-stitch square working on the impressionist painting cross-stitch project as the afternoon wore on. I was beginning to feel like all of Tallulah Falls had turned in for an early nap and that I was the only one who didn't get the text instituting the new policy. There wasn't even that much traffic on the sidewalk.

"Maybe I'm just lonely without Angus here," I said to Jill, the mannequin who is a dead ringer for Marilyn Monroe. "What do you think?"

She figured that was probably it—along with the fact that I was concerned about the Movie Murder Madness. Was that a good name for it?

"It's as good as any, I suppose," I said. Before you think I went entirely off my rocker, I was fully aware that Jill could not actually communicate with me. But when a person is bored, she'll come up with all sorts of imaginative distractions.

"So, what's your take on this movie murder madness, Jill? Do you think the gunman's death is—as Ted suspects—tied in to the other two murders? Or is it completely coincidental that the gunman was killed near where Babs met her untimely death?"

Jill gave this some thought. She decided that we needed to deduce why each of the three victims was most likely killed.

"Good thinking," I said. "Let's start with the gunman. He was probably killed over a disagreement with his partner. No one has ever hinted at any other motive for his death."

Jill reminded me that I wasn't privy to all the information pertaining to that investigation but admitted that I was probably right. "Besides, we strongly suspect that the person leaving the area on the dirt bike was the gunman's partner, do we not?" I sometimes imagined Jill putting a proper, Jane-Austen-y spin on her phrases.

"We *do* suspect that, Jill. Or, we might call the person on the dirt bike—as Deputy Preston pointed out—a mud slinger. I thought that was a clever moniker, didn't you?"

"Indeed," I imagined Jill responding. "And he had a similar button, which we now know to be a medallion, to the one Vera found. So now I'm wondering if the two men knew each other . . . if perhaps they were in the same mud slinging club."

"I wondered that too, but if you'll recall, I asked Deputy Preston about it. He denied knowing the young man."

"He did. . . . Let's move on to Babushka Tru. Why would someone want to kill her?"

"You mean, besides the fact that she was as mean as a snake?" I asked Jill.

"Now, now. . . . There simply has to be a better reason than that, or else there would be no hateful people in the world. And as I stand here immobile watching the public come and go, I realize that hateful people—even people as hateful as Babushka Tru—are allowed to remain alive all the time."

Jill had an excellent point. Most often, our desire to stay out of prison is much stronger than our desire to strike a hateful person, even if we don't intend the strike to result in said person falling off a ledge to her death.

"Jill, you've got me talking like you," I said. I sighed and resumed stitching.

But Jill insisted we weren't done. We needed to dig for the deeper motive behind Babs' death.

"If it wasn't out of sheer exasperation on the part of someone she was haranguing, then it had to have been because someone wanted her out of the picture . . . meaning the film—get it? Or it had to be that she saw something she shouldn't have seen," I mused. "Let's say Ted is right in his assumption that Babs' death is tied to the gunman's death. She must've found some sort of evidence that pointed to the killer, or she might've connected him to the gunman."

Jill pointed out that Babs' phone had gone missing and that during that time two of Babs' financial accounts had been hacked.

"What if Babs had learned who'd had her phone?" I wondered aloud. "Then she would've known who'd hacked her accounts. She'd have filed a police report, and the thief and his new computer hacker would have been in deep. That could be the motive."

And what about Henry? Jill still didn't see why he'd been murdered, and frankly, neither did I.

Could Henry have been killed over something—or someone—he saw with Babs? Mom had said she spotted Henry heading in Babs' direction after she left the young diva that morning. Maybe Henry saw her with the killer.

But Henry was Babs' father. He wouldn't just let someone hit her on the head and knock her off the edge of the loft. And if he had witnessed the murder, he'd have surely reported what he'd seen.

I stitched while I contemplated Henry's death. Finally, I came to two conclusions: he could have reported what he'd seen to Detectives Bailey and Ray and they'd sworn him to silence; or Henry might not have seen a thing, but the killer thought he did.

I giggled. "Maybe the killer is Deputy Preston, Jill. He's a mud slinger, so it could've very well been him on the dirt bike leaving the scene of the first murder. And he was in Henry's hotel room just before Sonny arrived. . . ." My voice trailed off, and my smile faded. The thought of Deputy Preston being the murderer wasn't as far-fetched as it had first seemed.

I placed my cross-stitch project on the coffee table as I stood. As I walked into my office to get my laptop, I was wondering why the cyanide had taken so long to affect Henry. If Deputy Preston had, in fact, poisoned Henry, wouldn't Henry have been dead when Sonny arrived? Before I rushed to judgment, I needed to know the answer to that question.

I searched one webpage after another. Frankly, I was beginning to fear that federal agents would burst into the Seven-Year Stitch at any moment and order me to step away from the computer with my hands up. Looking up all this information on poisons had to be a red flag to someone.

Then I found it—a Dr. Lyle had blogged about the length of time it would take for cyanide to affect a victim. The doctor had concluded that the length of time for the poison to affect the victim would depend upon the size of the dosage and whether or not the victim ingested the poison on a full or empty stomach. Dr. Lyle explained that after ingestion, the sodium or potassium cyanide reacts with stomach acids to form hydrogen cyanide in the stomach. The hydrogen cyanide is rapidly absorbed and kills the victim. However, in a full stomach, the acid would be diluted by the food and delay the reaction time.

I recalled Mom saying that Henry's breakfast tray had been on the table by the window. If Deputy Preston had come along with the poison just after Henry had finished eating and maybe added the cyanide to Henry's coffee, then that would explain how Henry was still alive when Sonny came to visit.

Sonny told me that Henry was jittery, sweating and breathing hard. He also said Henry kept putting his hands up to his temples as if he had a headache. I did a search for symptoms of cyanide poisoning—even though I knew the cause of death—just to make sure these were the stages Henry would've gone through before death.

So now I had deemed Deputy Preston a plausible suspect. It made perfect sense. He was attending the same junior college as the gunman. They could've either met there or been friends before enrolling in the school. Either way, when Preston had lost his first hacker—the gunman—he could've simply recruited another . . . unless, of course, there had been more than one hacker in the group to begin with.

When the movie crew came to Tallulah County to film, Deputy Preston saw the opportunity as too lucrative to pass up. From what I'd seen of Babushka Tru, I could imagine her leaving her phone lying around and then screeching orders for someone to find it. Plus, she was flirtatious, and Deputy Preston was a nice-looking guy. And I'd even seen him in the outtake footage—proof that he'd gotten close to the star.

But what would be his motive for killing Henry? And where would he have gotten the cyanide?

I put my head against the chair and stared up at the ceiling. What had Detective Ray said before he was aware I was standing in the kitchen? He'd said something about Henry's poisoning being only the second cyanide poisoning the Tallulah County Police Department had investigated in five years. If the police department had not only investigated, but had gathered evidence and made an arrest, then wouldn't the poison be stored in an evidence room or something?

I decided to call Ted and find out. My call went to voice mail so I left a message: "Hi. I need to ask you something. How long is evidence kept? In particular, I'm wondering if the Tallulah County Police Department would still have evidence from a five-year-old case. Please find out and give me a call. I want to run a hunch past you."

I shut down my laptop and returned to the sit-and-stitch square to resume work on the Monet. I was thinking *oh, my gosh, it really could be Deputy Preston! He could really be the killer!*

And then all of a sudden I was thinking of Sonny. Even if it was an outrageous theory and the killer turned out not to be Deputy Preston after all, shouldn't I call and warn Sonny? After all, Deputy Preston—or the killer, no matter who he or she might be—could make the assumption that Henry had said something to Sonny that would be incriminating. Wouldn't that put Sonny's life in danger as well?

I was rising to get my cell phone out of my pocket when the bells over the shop door alerted me to the fact that I had a visitor. Too bad the visitor turned out to be Deputy Preston.

I was so afraid my face had given me away, even though I tried to unwiden my eyes and lower my brows and pretend that everything was hunky-dory fine.

"Hey!" I said as brightly as I could. "What brings you back by today?"

Deputy Preston looked grave. "It's your mom, Marcy. There's been an attempt on her life, and I need to take you to her right away."

"Really?" No way was I buying that. I took the

phone from my pocket. "Let me call Ted. He can be over at my house faster than we can get there."

"She's not at the house," he said.

"Where is she?" I asked.

"She'd gone for a walk on the beach."

"What happened to her?"

"I don't know," Deputy Preston said quickly. "Detective Ray didn't give me all the details."

I frowned. "Why did he call you in on your day off if he wasn't going to tell you what was going on?"

The officer's face hardened. "Put the phone on the counter, Marcy. You're coming with me."

"I don't think that's such a good idea," I said.

He took a revolver from his pocket. "I don't care what you think. You and I are going for a ride."

He had me there. Rock beats scissors. Scissors cuts paper. Paper covers rock. Truth defeats darkness. Revolver trounces truth.

"Why'd you kill Babs and Henry?" I asked.

"Come on. Put the phone on the counter and walk slowly toward me."

This time I did as he asked. I needed to figure out a plan, but I was going to have to think outside of the comfort zone of the Seven-Year Stitch. I looked at Jill and gave her a silent good-bye. I imagined her quoting her doppelganger: Dogs never bite me. Just humans.

Amen, sister.

Deputy Preston grabbed my upper arm and propelled me toward the door. I looked up, down, and across the street. Surely, if Sadie, Blake, Todd, or even the mean old aromatherapy shop owner saw me, they'd know something wasn't right.

"Can I lock up?" I asked. "I don't want the shop to be burglarized."

"Leave it. Getting robbed is the least of your problems."

I nodded.

He pulled me along to his car—a blue, four-door Saturn sedan—and opened the passenger-side door. Before I got in, I looked through the back window. Sonny Carlisle had been bound and gagged and was lying on the seat. I gasped.

"Yeah, say hello to your good friend Sonny," Deputy Preston said. "Now get in."

I got into the car. Sonny had met my eyes, and I'd read the fear and dread in his face that I realized had probably been mirrored in my own. Judging by the bruise forming on the right side of his face, Sonny had taken a hard hit. I wondered if he'd been knocked unconscious. Sonny was a big guy. He could've held his own with Deputy Preston in a fair fight.

"Where are we going?" I asked.

"You ask a lot of questions. You know that?" He

turned on the ignition, put the car in reverse, and backed out into traffic.

Could I cause him to wreck the car? Probably not without getting myself shot and possibly hurting someone innocent. Despite the lack of foot traffic on the sidewalk, there were still plenty of people on the streets. Maybe I could make Deputy Preston lose control of the car when we got onto a more deserted stretch of road.

"You still haven't answered the first question I asked you," I said. "Why did you kill Henry and Babs?"

"Just shut up. I don't want to have to kill you in my car."

Sonny somehow managed to kick the back of my seat. I didn't know if he was warning me to be quiet or trying to reassure me that he had a plan. If it was the first one, I heeded the warning . . . but I hoped the kick was signaling the latter.

Chapter Twenty-five

As Deputy Preston sped down the highway toward the movie location, I tried to remain calm and assess the situation. Since I was in the front seat with the deputy, he was watching every move I made. Any attempt to open the door and jump out could be thwarted or could otherwise end badly. I could be run over by the car or shot by Deputy Preston.

Sonny was also unlikely to make a successful escape. Even if we stopped at a traffic light and he managed to open the back door and roll out of the car, it's unlikely he'd even be able to get to his feet before Deputy Preston sped away. As in my escape scenario, this could result in Sonny being run over by either the Saturn or another vehicle. Besides, I had no idea whether or not Sonny was even weighing his escape options.

What other recourse did I have? I could wait until Deputy Preston stopped the car and got out, but that was risky. What if he made me get out first, kept the gun trained on me, and then followed me out the passenger side? But if he *didn't* make me get out first, and if he got out but kept the gun on me, I could maybe put my leg over like I was getting out and then press the gas and take off, thus saving myself and Sonny. No . . . the fact that Deputy Preston was more than a foot taller than me meant that I'd have to slide nearly under the dashboard to be able to both reach the gas pedal and avoid the bullet the crazy officer was sure to fire.

And then it hit me like a wave of nausea. Actually, it *was* a wave of nausea, which is what made my acting so believable.

"I'm gonna be sick," I said, heaving dramatically over Deputy Preston.

"Don't you dare puke on me," he said.

"I . . . can't. . . ." I gagged again. "Can't help it. . . ."

He pulled over to the side of the road and stopped the car. When he did, Sonny brought up his bound fists and smashed Deputy Preston over the head. I pushed the gun away from me. The gun discharged and shot through the front of the car. Sonny continued clubbing Deputy Preston over the head. Despite being moderately incapacitated, Sonny was doing a decent job.

I bit the officer's wrist in an attempt to make

him drop the gun. He didn't drop the gun; he brought his wrist up and hit me in the mouth. I still held his arm with both hands.

Sonny made a sound that I later learned was supposed to be "Run!" With the gag in his mouth, I couldn't understand the command. I wouldn't have obeyed it anyway, because I wouldn't have left Sonny alone with a killer. One, it wouldn't have been the honorable thing to do. Two, the most likely outcome of my running was that Deputy Preston would first shoot me and then turn and finish off Sonny, dumping us both out there on the side of the road like garbage bags waiting to be picked up by jailhouse trustees.

After hearing Sonny's muffled cry, the next sound I heard was a keening wail. I considered that Sonny might be screaming. . . . Or I might be. . . . Was it *me* making that sound? No. No, thank God, it was sirens. Help was here.

Ted had received my message and had driven to the shop. Finding the door unlocked, no cardboard clock announcing when I'd return, and me nowhere in the building had sent his alarm bells into overdrive. He'd already come to the same conclusion I had about the possibility of Deputy Preston being the murderer. He'd called Detectives Ray and Bailey. He explained his theory that

Deputy Preston had been integral in the hacking and theft ring and that he believed the deputy had not only murdered Babushka Tru and Henry Beaumont but that I could be his next victim.

It just so happened that Detectives Bailey and Ray were on that same track themselves. The fact that Deputy Preston had asked to work extra shifts at the initial crime scene and then at the movie set had raised red flags with them. When searches of my property and Sonny Carlisle's hotel room didn't turn up any products containing cyanide, they'd checked the evidence logged on the earlier case and found that the container had been tampered with and that some of the poison had been taken. As soon as they got the call from Ted, they'd put out an all-points bulletin (APB) on Deputy Preston's personal vehicle. Ted, guessing Deputy Preston would take me to the original crime scene, was already en route there when he was joined by Detectives Bailey and Ray.

Detectives Bailey and Ray later informed Manu— who told Ted, who told me—that Deputy Preston had confessed to killing Babs after she deduced he'd taken her cell phone. It seems that although she might have been malicious, spiteful, and disrespect-ful, she was not stupid. No one among the movie cast or crew would have stolen her phone and then hacked into her accounts. Had they had that inten-tion, they'd have done it while they were still in San Francisco. She knew it had to be her latest conquest,

Deputy Preston. He'd been at her beck and call, and she was furious when she realized that his attention had been a ruse to get her financial information. When she confronted him, he hit her in the back of the head with a two-by-four and knocked her to her death.

As Deputy Preston was walking away from the crime scene, he met Henry. He stopped Henry and asked if he'd heard anything. Henry said no, but Deputy Preston insisted he'd heard something from the direction of the loft. Together, they went and "found" Babs' body. When he got home from work that evening and took off his uniform, Deputy Preston noticed a small amount of blood on his right sleeve. He began to wonder if Henry doubted the story of his hearing something from the loft, so he made it a point to watch Henry closely. He eventually convinced himself that Henry did, indeed, suspect him, so he murdered Henry.

With regard to Sonny and me, Deputy Preston planned to set Sonny up to look like the murderer. He had the rest of the cyanide he'd taken from the evidence room, and he'd planned to plant it on Sonny's body after Sonny and I were dead. He thought he could shoot me, shoot Sonny, and then put the gun in Sonny's hand—the intention being that everyone would think I'd caught on to Sonny's nefarious deeds, confronted him, and that he'd killed me and then killed himself.

Sonny said that was the stupidest thing he'd ever heard. If he was the killer, why would he murder me—the last remaining loose end—and then turn the gun on himself. No screenwriter worth his salt would write such a thing, and no detective would believe it. Ted agreed with that last part.

Carl Paxton was devastated to learn that Babs had been pregnant and that he was the father of her child. Rather than take on Mita Trublonski as a client, he canceled the tell-all book. The last Mom heard, he'd left Hollywood and returned to his hometown somewhere in the Midwest where he'd become an insurance salesman.

A couple days after what she referred to as "the incident," Mom returned home to San Francisco. She quickly found a new movie needing an expert costume designer. The new movie didn't have any buzz about any huge awards, but Mom decided she didn't want the media to pay close attention to her ever again. If need be, she could live without accolades. I knew she was deluding herself, but for the time being, it was what she needed to do. She did tell me the last time we talked that she'd been doodling a little on that clothing line.

It took a little while for my mouth to heal. Fortunately, I didn't lose any teeth or suffer any scarring, or any of that jazz. Ted had to be especially tender when kissing me for a couple days, but that was okay.

ACKNOWLEDGMENTS

As always, I must thank God first and foremost. I also thank my beautiful family—Tim, Lianna, and Nicholas. Thanks to Cooper for being my furry therapist. I'd like to thank my editor, Jessica Wade, my agent, Robert Gottlieb, and his assistant, Adrienne Lombardo.

Special thanks go out to Laurent Legendre of Le P'tit Laurent in San Francisco, who graciously allowed his restaurant to be featured in this book; and to D. P. Lyle, MD, author of *The Writer's Forensics Blog*, award-winning novelist and television consultant.

ABOUT THE AUTHOR

Amanda Lee lives in southwest Virginia with her husband and two beautiful children, a boy and a girl. She's a full-time writer/editor/mom/wife and chief cook and bottle washer, and she loves every minute of it. Okay, not the bottle washing so much, but the rest of it is great.

CONNECT ONLINE

www.gayletrent.com
www.facebook.com/gayletrentandamandalee
twitter.com/gayletrent